"MY FRIENDS CALL ME COWBOY."

She gave him what she hoped was her most polite, most disinterested smile. "Well then, Cowboy, now that you've sobered up, you'd better get on your way. I'm trying to run a business here and—"

"Sobered up? Look, angel-face, I tried to tell you I'm not drunk."

Angel-face? Martinique felt her chest squeeze tight. She didn't want him to call her that. She didn't like the way it made her feel. She gave him a skeptical frown. "I found you passed out in the gutter. Passed out and reeking of some very strong, very cheap whiskey. How do you explain that?"

He ran a hand across his eyes, then looked over at her with a tough, take-it-or-leave-it kind of expression. "Bad judgment."

He reached a hand out and tilted her chin toward him. Martinique felt the rough calluses trace across the delicate surface of her skin, like coarse leather against cream silk. It was a gentle touch, but insistent, erotic. Martinique instantly understood what kind of lover he would be. Slow, ruthless, and very sure of himself. Sure of the way a woman would respond to him.

His deep-water eyes stared straight into hers. "Ms. Martinique Duval, if I'm not mistaken. Just the lady I've been looking for. But don't worry, angel-face. You're the kind of woman a man remembers in his dreams. I couldn't forget you if I wanted to."

WHAT ARE *LOVESWEPT* ROMANCES?

They are stories of true romance and touching emotion. We believe those two very important ingredients are constants in our highly sensual and very believable stories in the LOVE-SWEPT line. Our goal is to give you, the reader, stories of consistently high quality that may sometimes make you laugh, sometimes make you cry, but are always fresh and creative and contain many delightful surprises within their pages.

Most romance fans read an enormous number of books. Those they truly love, they keep. Others may be traded with friends and soon forgotten. We hope that each LOVESWEPT romance will be a treasure—a "keeper." We will always try to publish

LOVE STORIES YOU'LL NEVER FORGET BY AUTHORS YOU'LL ALWAYS REMEMBER

The Editors

Loveswept ®
819

HERO
FOR HIRE

CYNTHIA
POWELL

BANTAM BOOKS
NEW YORK · TORONTO · LONDON · SYDNEY · AUCKLAND

HERO FOR HIRE

A Bantam Book / January 1997

ISBN 0-553-44549-9

Published simultaneously in the United States and Canada

Bantam Books are published by Bantam Books, a division of Bantam Doubleday Dell Publishing Group, Inc. Its trademark, consisting of the words "Bantam Books" and the portrayal of a rooster, is Registered in U.S. Patent and Trademark Office and in other countries. Marca Registrada. Bantam Books, 1540 Broadway, New York, New York 10036.

PRINTED IN THE UNITED STATES OF AMERICA

OPM   0 9 8 7 6 5 4 3 2 1

ONE

Cade C. Jackson knew a hundred ways to start a barroom brawl. When he walked into the Bourbon Street Boozery, the dive du jour for low-life French Quarter criminals, he hoped he wouldn't have to use them. But Cade knew from experience that a good fight might be the only way to make the New Orleans swamp scum spill their guts.

He ordered an ice-cold brew from the bartender, dropped a five on the counter, and tossed his drink back in one sweet, easy swallow. Declining a refill, he walked past a table of the biggest, baddest beer-belching street bikers he'd ever seen, made his way to the jukebox, and, with a quick, reckless yank, pulled the plug from its socket.

The music stopped. Cade waited. Two seconds later all eyes were focused on him.

"Man, are you crazy?" the bartender asked.

When the lead biker rose from his chair, three hundred pissed-off pounds of enormous and ugly, with tattoos quivering and nostrils flaring, Cade realized he'd passed crazy long ago.

"Hey, ratbrain," the biker grunted, drawing a switchblade from his jeans and cocking open the eight-inch steel cutting edge, "that was my favorite song. And if you can't sing as good as Meatloaf, you'd better know how to fight dirty, run fast, or pray hard."

A series of drunken hoots and howls followed this brilliant speech. Mr. Big, Bad and Born to Be Wild turned to his audience and grinned. And Cade followed rule number three from Cowboy Jackson's Personal Guide to Street Survival. *Never pass up an opportunity.*

He grabbed Big Boy by the back of the head, latched onto his long, leather-tied ponytail, and twisted hard. The knife clattered to the ground as the biker writhed and roared with pain, but Cade refused to let go. He lifted an oyster knife from the table with his free hand and positioned it at the base of Big Boy's greasy scalp.

"Sit down, dipstick, or I'm taking your hair as a souvenir."

The hoots and hollers around the room were on Cade's side this time.

Big Boy sat down. "Easy there, man, it took four years to grow! What the hell do you want anyway?"

Cade released his grip on the ponytail, planted the knife tip in the tabletop, and spoke to the crowd that had gathered around him. "Information." He pulled a sketch from the back pocket of his jeans and passed it around the room. "All I want is a little information. . . ."

❧————————❧

Half an hour later Cade was walking down Royal Street, scanning the expensive clutter of elegant store-front windows for the right address. He stopped outside a two-story brick building and squinted up at the street number in the fading light. *Heirloom Antiques* was painted in flowing script letters across the glass window, framing a display of upscale art, old-time furniture, and fancy bric-a-brac. A Closed sign was tucked into the lower left corner, wedged between the slender marble statue of a woman and the tasseled silk shade of a painted porcelain lamp.

Cade didn't bother trying the door, but checked out the courtyard entrance, where a tall narrow gate of black wrought iron led to a small, secluded patio. The gate was locked, but he heard the faint sound of falling water, caught the seductive scent of night-blooming jasmine, and saw the erotic shape of a woman moving in the cool, green courtyard beyond.

Fascinated, Cade moved in for a closer look.

And liked what he saw. Fine, faintly exotic features, a tumble of loose hair that just grazed her slender shoulders, creamy, suntanned skin the color of café au lait. But what interested him the most was the way her summer-white cotton robe clung to the sleek curves of her body. It was cinched at the waist with a ribbon-sized belt, leaving a wide triangle of skin exposed above the navel and only a few tempting inches hidden from his sight.

Even without those few inches, Cade decided the

view was still a good one. Her breasts were full and unbound, with only that thin layer of cotton covering the dark outline of her nipples. She was tending to some plants, a watering can in her hand, and every time she leaned over, Cade swore the fabric was about to give way. Hell, he was praying for it.

Then she knelt down onto the ground, and the bottom half of the robe fell away, baring slim ankles, long legs, and the most sinfully sweet thighs a man could imagine. Cade wanted to check the number over the door again, to make sure he had the right address, but he couldn't seem to tear his eyes away. He wasn't even sure he wanted to know.

It was part of his job to track down and talk to one Martinique Duval. According to the police report, she was the woman who'd last seen his quarry. As far as he knew, she was the only person who could make a positive ID on the perpetrator and lead him to the lowlife he was searching for. But instead of ringing the buzzer and introducing himself, he was spying on her in her own backyard.

If this woman wasn't Ms. Duval, he'd have a helluva time explaining his presence here. And if she *was* Ms. Duval, he knew he was in for a helluva lot of trouble.

Cade started to realize just how much trouble when the blow came from behind. He felt a crack against his skull, a sharp pain, then the soothing warmth of a liquid, wet and sticky, dripping down his temples. The last thing he saw before blacking out was the woman in white, walking back into her house.

Cade decided that whoever she was, it was a dirty shame he wouldn't live long enough to meet her.

Martinique Duval unlocked the heavy iron gate, pushed it wide, and rolled her trash can through to the usual pick-up spot at the curb. Yawning, she glanced up Royal Street to make sure the garbage truck hadn't already come. Judging from the other cans and bags lined up and down the long row of narrow, balconied buildings, she figured she'd made it in time for the early-morning collection. She turned back to her courtyard apartment as Ming and Ching, her two adopted alley cats, darted through the open gate and out onto the street curb.

Martinique groaned. It was too early to be chasing a pair of wayward pranksters all over the French Quarter, especially when she was still wearing her robe and nightgown and hadn't even had her first sip of coffee.

"Get back here, you little hooligans."

But Ming and Ching weren't paying her the slightest bit of attention. They were too busy inspecting the sidewalk, dashing from one trash can to the next, nosing around for anything that smelled the least bit interesting. Ming headed for a furniture truck parked at the curb and scrambled around the front of it and out of view. At the sound of her soft meow, Ching followed.

Martinique sighed, took a few steps forward around the front of the truck, and saw immediately what her cats had found so fascinating. Lying face down in the gutter, with his booted legs sprawled on the sidewalk and his dark head positioned precariously at the edge of the street, was the body of a man.

Martinique stared down at him, disgust and pity rising in her heart. Another street bum. The French Quarter had more than its fair share of them, an unhappy side effect of the wall-to-wall bars, nightclubs, and strip clubs along Bourbon Street. Thanks to the constant flow of beer and booze until the early-morning hours, this wasn't the first drunk who'd decided to lie down and sleep it off on her sidewalk.

But this one had picked an especially inconvenient spot. As soon as the city woke up and traffic started rolling again, he was liable to get his head run over. Martinique stepped forward and cautiously nudged him in the side with the toe of her satin house slipper.

He didn't move.

Ming and Ching scurried along the length of him, sniffing. Martinique frowned and it occurred to her that maybe he'd overdosed on alcohol and drunk himself to death.

She swallowed against a painful lump in her throat. She'd witnessed that before as well, only last time, the victim hadn't been a stranger.

Pushing away the unwelcome memory, she bent down and tried to determine if he was breathing. The stale scent of whiskey drifted up to her, mingled with the putrid odor of the previous night's garbage. The combination nearly made her gag, but she held her breath, bent her head close to his, and listened for the steady intake of air.

It was faint but audible. She exhaled in relief. At least he wasn't dead.

But then she noticed the blood.

It was rust red, caked and matted against the long strands of his chicory black hair. It started from a small gash at the top of his scalp, streaked across the dark waves, and ended in a sticky smear along the hard outline of his temple. Martinique swore softly. The injury didn't look life threatening, but just to be on the safe side, she ought to call an ambulance. But first she'd have to move him.

And she didn't like the idea one bit. If he had a serious head injury, she might end up hurting him more. But if she left him in the street, he could end up a lot worse. Even if the driver of the furniture truck managed to avoid him, the next car to come along would make jambalaya out of his brains.

She was still exploring the options when her housekeeper rounded the corner and methodically made her way up the street. Ming and Ching instantly abandoned the motionless body and ran to greet Adora, a sure and steady source of their favorite food. They bunched themselves at her ankles, circling and nosing affectionately against her wine-dark skin.

Martinique smiled. "Thank God."

Adora bent down to stroke Ming and Ching, then stood up again, statuesque in her flowing dress of silk batik. She glared down at the man in the gutter, scowling. "Bah," she said, and spat on the sidewalk. "A bum."

Martinique nodded. "He's hurt. I think he needs help."

Adora shook her head ominously, her gold hoop earrings flashing in the early light. "Ha! Hurt himself, I say. Too much drink. Man like that—the body is ruined. The soul beyond help. Leave it alone, Nikki."

Martinique bit her lower lip. She might have known Adora would start to get stubborn, and she really couldn't blame her. She wasn't exactly thrilled with the situation herself. He wasn't her problem, after all. She wished she could just walk away, close the gate behind her, and leave the man to look after himself. But something inside her made the wish impossible. She just couldn't abandon the guy to his fate. Which more than likely would be a set of tire tracks across the skull.

Unless she could convince Adora to help her move him.

"You're right," she told the older woman calmly. "He probably is a basket case. I doubt anyone can save him."

Adora eyed her suspiciously. "Humph. Didn't say he *can't* be saved. Only said he ain't *worth* saving." She took a closer look at the man, her dark gaze sparkling with sudden professional interest.

Martinique smiled inwardly. Adora's instincts as a holistic healer were fully engaged. Her spiritual background combined beliefs from Caribbean, African, and Creole French cultures in a mystical melting pot that was typically New Orleans. Her metaphysical and medicinal talents were said to be strong. And the man in the gutter was a clear challenge to her reputation.

Adora laid a hand on his head where the blood was dark and damp from the morning mist. "There are ways . . ." she suggested, her voice soft and full of mystery.

She looked up at Martinique, and when their eyes met, they both laughed. "Wicked!" Adora said. "The *orisas* will punish you for outsmarting a poor old woman."

Martinique grinned back. "A poor old woman who looks like a queen and talks so fierce that even the alligators are afraid of her? A woman who—"

"Never you mind, Nikki!" Adora interjected, her eyes flashing with pleasure at the compliment. "You take hold of his arms and I will lift from the other end."

Martinique nodded and they positioned themselves at opposite ends of the body. Together they managed to roll him onto his back, but the smell was so strong that Martinique had to turn her face away. Gritting her teeth, she latched onto his shoulders and pulled with everything she had.

Unlike a lot of drunks she'd seen on the street, this one wasn't emaciated from lack of food. He was one solid mass of hard-packed muscle, as heavy and unyielding as the bronze statue in her shop. A groaning sound escaped her as tiny beads of sweat tickled at the nape of her neck. It was just her luck to get saddled with a well-built bum.

Mr. August, she decided ruefully. *The bum of the month. Hobbies include pub-crawling and guzzling large shots of straight whiskey. Favorite sport: gutter napping.*

She took a deep breath and let it out again in a long sigh. It was such a waste. Especially for a man who appeared to be in the prime of life. If he ever got himself hosed off and sobered up, he could become a strong, productive citizen. Unfortunately, all that dead weight made him about as easy to carry as the proverbial ton of bricks.

Luckily, they didn't have far to go. Within a few minutes they'd hauled him safely away from the curb and dragged him deep into the shaded seclusion of the courtyard. Ming and Ching followed, loath to miss any of the morning's excitement. Martinique sank down onto the moss-covered bricks and gingerly positioned the stranger's head in her lap. She didn't want to touch him any more than was absolutely necessary, but she couldn't very well drop him on the ground and expose his open wound to the hard surface.

"We ought to call an ambulance," she said, looking up at Adora with growing concern. "All that jostling and he still hasn't come around. And he's shivering," she added, feeling a faint trembling along the stranger's bare arms.

"From the damp," Adora reasoned. "You'd be shivering too, girl, if you'd had nothin' but a cold slab of concrete for a bed. That boy needs a blanket." She latched the gate, then made her way up the curved iron staircase to the second floor of the apartment, disappearing inside.

Alone with the stranger, Martinique tried to think of anything except the way he smelled of stale whiskey and how many diseases he was probably carrying. Then, looking down at his face for the first time, she felt something stir inside her and realized that something was a strong sense of shock.

Mr. August had more than just another great body. He had high, chiseled cheekbones angling down to a square, stubborn jaw. He had a perfect nose, except for that single, rugged bump where it had probably been broken long ago. He had dark, upswept eyebrows, a firm, compelling mouth and skin as smooth and tan as bayou bourbon.

It was an insolent face. Uncompromising. Men would move aside and give him room. Women would stare at him and make wishes too private to reveal.

Other women, Martinique decided. Not her. She was too familiar with men of his sort. Men who would take their pleasure and leave nothing behind except heartache. Tough guys who liked their whiskey strong and their women weak.

But Martinique was not weak. And rough, dangerous men held no thrill for her. Not even one with a fascinating face. A face too hard to be handsome.

Martinique reached down to brush away a strand of dark hair from his forehead, but stopped herself short. What was she doing? Only moments before, the thought of touching him had filled her with disgust. And now she could barely keep the instinct to comfort him at bay. The instinct to run her fingers along the hard planes of his face, to tangle them in the streaming blackness of his hair. She curled her hand carefully into a tight ball and held it there.

Only Ming and Ching didn't seem averse to touching the stranger. With the temptations of the street beyond their reach, they settled down to explore this new creature as thoroughly as their small, wet noses would allow. Ming was the more cautious of the two and kept her whiskers at least an inch away from the dormant body. A cat never knew when something that large might wake up and make a sudden move.

Ching was anything but shy. And he didn't appreciate having a strange male invading what he considered his personal territory. So just to get the message across, he sauntered up to the stranger's side, turned around, and sprayed the man's bare arm with a warm and steady stream of cat urine.

Cade's first conscious feeling was the faint sensation of a liquid, warm and dribbling against his arm. It trickled down around his elbow, running in a tiny, tickling rivulet toward his wrist. He wondered if the woman in bed with him was playing some kind of kinky sex game. Not that he would object, but he wasn't sure if he had the energy for it this morning. It must've been one rowdy, righteous party last night if he was waking up in such poor condition. Too bad he couldn't remember it. Too bad he couldn't remember her name.

Struggling against a dark wall of sleep, he fought hard to open his eyes. He blinked them open for a second, but closed them just as quickly against the bright morning light. *Morning light?* Where the hell was he, anyway?

And then he started to remember. Someone had snuck up on him from behind and nearly bashed his brains out. Someone had tried to kill him. And based on the stiff, chilling numbness in his body, he figured that they must've succeeded. He'd cashed in his chips for sure this time. Arm-wrestled with the grim reaper and lost. Cowboy Jackson was dead as a swamp rat in a rattlesnake's belly.

He opened his eyes again, more cautiously this time, and realized that somehow, somewhere, someone had made a big mistake and actually sent him to heaven. How else could he explain the incredible vision floating before his eyes? It was a woman looking down at him with an emotion he barely recognized. Genuine concern. It was a woman with the face of an angel.

His head was cradled in her lap and he was staring up into the sweetest, sexiest green eyes he'd ever seen. Her hair was soft and full, her features sleek and elegant, her lips designed by divine inspiration. Hell yes, it *had* to be an angel, because nothing on earth had ever looked so good.

And then a sudden, unwelcome thought filtered through to his noncorporeal consciousness. Maybe she wasn't real after all. Maybe he was having some kind of weird, brain-dead delusion. The wise thing to do would be just to lie back and enjoy it. But Cade rarely did the wise thing. He was used to living dangerously. He put a hand up to touch her.

Angel-face pushed his hand away. "Not in a million years, mister."

Cade frowned, slightly puzzled. That sounded more like a response he might've gotten in real life. And the simple movement of his hand had somehow made his head start to throb. The blood was pulsing in his ears, the pain so sharp it made him want to retch. Did they have headaches in heaven? Or was God playing some cosmic joke on him before shipping him south? He reached up to feel the back of his head, groaned, and lowered his arm again.

"Hold still," Angel-face told him. "Adora is coming with a blanket to cover you." She put a delicate hand up to her nose and added, "Although we'll probably have to burn it afterwards."

Cade blinked in confusion. Definitely not angel talk. He swallowed thickly and, through sheer determination, actually got his mouth to speak. "What's that supposed to mean?"

She looked down at him with those gorgeous green eyes and wrinkled her nose in distaste. "It means you *stink.*"

Cade finally came down to earth. Yup, it was getting more and more like the real world he remembered. The tough world. The one he knew more about than he really cared to.

He took a deep breath and finally got a good whiff of himself. Damned if Angel-face wasn't right. He had the distinct odor of a sewer rat who'd slept in a puddle of pond scum. His mouth tasted as bad as gator breath. And the combination was starting to make his stomach roil.

He took another gulp of air and prayed he'd have the self-control to keep from puking in Angel-face's lap. Unfortunately, his prayers were seldom answered.

"Sorry about this, sweetheart," he told her, deciding that some kind of advance warning would probably be a good idea, "but I'm about to lose my breakfast." Then he turned his head away and quietly tossed his cookies onto the courtyard bricks.

Surprisingly, he felt better almost immediately. Equally surprising was Angel-face's reaction. She didn't look like she exactly appreciated it, but she didn't dump his head on the ground, either. A real lady.

Even better than an angel, because her body was warm and real, her breasts round and full beneath the thin film of her nightgown. A vision that could tempt a man to sweet sin on a Sunday.

Cade struggled to sit up. Lying in the lady's lap wasn't hard to take, but it wasn't exactly helping his situation. A man could get used to something soft and sweet like that. So used to it, a man might never want to leave. And for a beat-up bounty hunter who made his living on the road, it was never wise to stick around too long.

It would be smart just to get the information and go. He'd make his move any second now. As soon as he could get his head to stop spinning. As soon as he could make the world hold still. Gritting his teeth, he hauled himself into a sitting position, let out a low groan, and put his head between his knees.

Martinique looked up in relief as her housekeeper called down from the top of the courtyard stairs. "So, he decides to join the living again, eh?" Adora asked, making her way toward Martinique and the stranger. Her arms were enveloped by a large blanket, and several small string-tied pouches trailed from her long fingertips. "Could be we don't want to waste this fine blanket and mojo bags on him, after all. How's about I just open the gate, Nikki, see if he can find his own way out?"

Martinique eyed the man skeptically, concern and resentment fighting for control of her heart. Why shouldn't they just open the gate and leave him to nurse his hangover alone? Because he's hurting bad, she told herself. Because he looks like the kind of man who wouldn't ask for help, no matter how badly he needed it.

"Maybe we should still call that ambulance," she suggested, thinking out loud.

Adora let out a low, rumbling laugh, deep and throaty. "Ambulance won't come for his kind! Too many poor drunks on the street to pick up. Too many who can't pay. Anyhow, he don't appear like he's hurt so bad. Just lost a little blood is all. Mojo bag'll take care of that." She set down the blanket, selected one small pouch from her assortment, and started to shake it over the stranger's head. Pale wisps of dust and tiny flakes of odd-smelling herbs floated down around his hair and shoulders.

"What the—" He lifted his head and squinted at Adora in irritation. "Leave me alone, woman! I'm not some drunk who needs saving with your swamp magic. And I sure as hell don't need an ambulance."

"Humph!" Adora grumbled, stepping back. "Devil!"

"You need to see a doctor," Martinique said quietly. "You're hurt."

She watched him pull away and gingerly touch the back of his scalp with one callused hand. "Been through worse," he told her. "And as long as my brains aren't spilling out the back, there's no way I'm settin' foot in any hospital. People die in hospitals. You check in for a little thing like this, and next thing you know, they're hanging a tag on your toe and slidin' you straight into a long steel icebox. No thank you, ma'am. I'd rather go it alone."

"Suit yourself," Martinique said coolly. "But next time you'd better pick another spot to pass out in. You nearly had your head caved in by a furniture truck. And a mess like that right in front of my shop could be very bad for business."

The stranger grinned at her as if he appreciated her hard-core humor. Martinique felt her temper rising. She hadn't wanted to make him smile. She'd wanted to make him leave. But he just sat there staring at her in open amusement, his eyes as blue and deep as a moonlit bayou, his grin as languid and lazy as a Louisiana summer.

He had the kind of smile that women made fools of themselves over. Uptown women would remove their masks at Mardi Gras, just to get a better look. Party girls would probably toss their panties at him. And he was the kind of man that would enjoy every minute of it. Crude, cocky, and way too sure of himself.

Martinique did not smile back. "Well then, since you seem to be feeling better, Mr. . . ."

"Jackson," he told her, running a strong hand speculatively across his unshaven jaw. "Cade Jackson. My friends call me Cowboy."

She gave him what she hoped was her most polite, most disinterested smile. "Well then, Mr. Jackson. Now that you've sobered up, you'd better get on your way. I'm trying to run a business here and—"

"Sobered up? Look, angel-face, I tried to tell Madam Witch Doctor here and I'll tell you again, I'm not drunk."

Angel-face? Martinique felt her chest squeeze tight. She didn't want him to call her that. She didn't like the way it made her feel. Even more annoying was the sudden, irrational hope that he was telling her the truth. The hope that she'd somehow misjudged him. But the evidence definitely didn't point in that direction.

She gave him a skeptical frown. "I found you passed out in the gutter. Passed out and reeking of some very strong, very cheap whiskey. How do you explain that?"

He ran a hand across his eyes, then looked over at her with a tough, take-it-or-leave-it kind of expression. "Bad judgment."

She folded her arms across her chest and gave him a wry smile. "I'll say."

"Listen, angel-face—"

"Don't call me that."

"Sure thing, sweetheart, but—"

"I am *not* your sweetheart. Try Ms. Duval. Think you're sober enough to remember that?"

He reached a hand out and tilted her chin toward him. Martinique felt the rough calluses trace across the delicate surface of her skin, like coarse leather against cream silk. It was a gentle touch, but insistent, erotic. Martinique instantly understood what kind of lover he would be. Slow, ruthless, and very sure of himself. Sure of the way a woman would respond to him.

His deep-water eyes stared straight into hers. "Ms. Martinique Duval, if I'm not mistaken. Just the lady I've been looking for. But don't worry, angel-face. You're the kind of woman a man remembers in his dreams. I couldn't forget you if I wanted to."

TWO

Martinique stared at the stranger in shock. No, she corrected herself, not exactly a stranger. She knew all about his type. He was bad news in blue jeans. Testosterone on tap. And she was *just the lady he'd been looking for.*

Well, Cade Jackson was just the kind of man she'd learned to avoid. The kind her mother had adored. Angelé had always had a weakness for racy, reckless lone-wolf types. Seductive, sweet-talking, fast-living losers. Come-and-go men who'd turned their tiny two-bedroom apartment above the French Quarter bar into the Creep-of-the-Month Club.

But Martinique didn't entirely blame Angelé for her vulnerability to beautiful bums. An attraction to men of the unmarrying kind was a genetic defect that all the Duval women shared. A fatal flaw that went back several generations.

Martinique's great-great-grandmother had been a mistress to French royalty. Her great-grandmother was remembered as a riverboat beauty of ill repute, with numerous admirers, one child, and no husband. Martinique's mother had followed in the family tradition, with a career tailor-made to her time. Angelé had been a stripper, mistress to any man with a handsome face and an aversion to commitment.

But her daughter was determined not to follow in their footsteps. And after twenty-eight years of careful, cautious living, she'd had plenty of practice.

"You . . . you know my name?" she asked quietly, willing herself to ignore the unwelcome emotions he'd stirred within her.

He really shouldn't be difficult to deal with. This was Gutter-man stroking her cheek here, not exactly the clean-cut prince of her dreams.

Cade finally dropped his hand from her face, but his eyes never wavered. "It's my business to know, angel-face."

"Exactly what sort of *business* are you in, Mr. Jackson?"

Several possibilities came to mind, but none of them were legal. The most legitimate career she could imagine for him was with the military. Something risky and gritty involving hair-triggered weapons, raging male hormones, and lots of weight lifting. But she couldn't quite picture him taking orders.

He stood up slowly, pulled a plain business card from the back pocket of his blue jeans and flipped it down to her. "I'm in the bounty-hunting business, Ms. Duval. I track down lowlifes, bail jumpers, burglars, petty thieves; I'm not particular as long as I get paid."

Adora let out a disbelieving laugh. "How you gonna catch a crook if you can't even find your own way home at night? Come into the house, Nikki. This Cowboy guy is up to no good. Probably rip you off like that holdup man last week who helped himself to your two best paintings."

Martinique moved over to the concrete garden bench and sat down to study the card. It didn't say much. Just gave Jackson's name, a phone number, and an obscure Acadiana address. For all the information it revealed, Adora could be right. Cade himself could be just another bad guy looking for some easy action. And she was fed up to the eyeballs with men who tried to steal away the comfort and security she'd fought so hard to achieve.

No one had handed her a successful antique business. No one had ever handed her anything. The shop she'd created was a small one, but it was well patronized, fashionable even, and it was all hers. She'd struggled her way to self-sufficiency, fended for herself, fought for her dreams. And nothing made her angrier than a criminal who thought it was his right to take something for nothing.

Martinique couldn't bring herself to believe that Jackson was that kind of man. After all, if he had any money, even other people's money, he'd be sleeping in a king-sized bed at the Royal Orleans instead of in her street. And how many holdup men introduced themselves before stealing you blind? Crooks like that didn't come with calling cards. The last one she'd encountered had come with a knife.

"It's all right, Adora. You can leave me alone with him. I think I need a cup of your coffee right now even more than your protection."

Adora made a move toward the house, but hesitated, still skeptical.

"Go on," Martinique scolded softly. "If he tries anything, I'll—" she paused, trying to think of something strong enough to stop Cade Jackson in his tracks, "I'll let him have it!" she finished lamely.

"Sounds interesting," he told her as soon as Adora had disappeared inside. "I thought sure you were the kind who'd play hard to get."

Martinique glared back at him. If being a bounty hunter took a lot of nerve, she'd bet Cade Jackson was the best in the business.

"And I thought someone who'd just been saved from certain death would at least have the decency to be grateful."

His grin widened and the sizzling blue eyes grew warm enough to melt stone. "Angel-face, I've been dreaming up ways to thank you all morning, but none of them are decent."

"Try leaving," she suggested politely, pointing to the gate.

But instead of obliging her, he whisked a heavy garden chair from under the magnolia tree, plopped it across from her, and settled himself into the seat. The chair was a few sizes too small and way too ornate for his solid masculine frame, but he still managed to look completely at home. Casually, he rubbed at a spot near the base of his arm, an ink-dark spot the dew hadn't washed away. He finally gave it up, lounged back, and gazed at her with a directness she found disconcerting.

"Send away a man who's just escaped certain death without so much as a cup of coffee? All that saving you did might go to waste. What if I pass out a second time and you have to rescue me all over again?"

Martinique eyed him doubtfully. Now that he was fully awake and very much in control of himself, Cade Jackson didn't look the least bit like he needed saving. And if any part of his brain had been damaged from the injury to his head, it was the section that governed civilized southern manners. The gray matter that contained boldness and sheer audacity was still perfectly intact.

She smiled sweetly. "Pass out again, Mr. Jackson, and you can spend eternity wearing tire tracks. Now, suppose you tell me what you're doing here. I don't have any crooks hiding out in my cellar for you to drag back and bring to justice. Other than that, I can't imagine what you'd want from me."

He leaned back in his chair, careless and cocksure as he studied her with interest. "Can't you?" he asked softly. "Well, I guess it's a good thing. I don't like having my face slapped. So I'd better stick to business."

"You'd better," she agreed.

"The scumbag who robbed your shop is the one I'm after."

Martinique blinked in surprise. "You know who stole my paintings?"

He nodded. "I know his M.O. He's a repeat offender. A career coward the law hasn't been able to catch. A coward with a hefty price on his head if I haul him in to the authorities." He hooked two thumbs along the rolled-up edges of his T-shirt sleeves and gave her a slow, self-satisfied smile. "And you, angel-face, are going to help me collect my reward."

She let out a short laugh, disbelieving. "Sure thing. Just give me a minute while I slip into the house for my sidearm and bulletproof vest."

"Nice of you to offer," he drawled, "but not necessary. I carry my own weapon." His tone was low and rusty, lethal. "Don't worry, I never fire it unless I have to. Unfortunately, dead criminals don't have any cash value. They're usually worthless unless I bring them back alive."

She shivered, a little awed by his blunt words because she knew he had the power to back them up. Brute strength rippled beneath those tight muscles, like molten lava straining against smooth, unyielding stone.

"How did you find me?" she asked, trying to steer the conversation onto safer ground. She needed facts, details, anything to bring her mind back to business.

"Police report," he said curtly. "The description you gave of your robber is an exact match for the perp I'm after. Better-than-average build, slicked-back, stringy brown hair, and a very tacky tattoo on his left arm. Remember what it said, sweetheart? *Bust My Buns.* Now that's what I call a cordial invitation. And I plan to take him up on the offer."

"And exactly how do you expect to accomplish what the entire New Orleans police force has been unable to do?" But even before the question was out, she knew the answer intuitively. This man was a law unto himself. After all he'd been through, he still looked unstoppable.

"Persistence, angel-face. It pays off."

"So where do I fit in?"

"You can fill in the blanks for me. You're the only eyewitness who's seen this guy in person." He pulled a small sketch from the pocket of his jeans and flashed it in front of her.

It was a copy of the police artist's drawing of the crook's face, pieced together, stroke by stroke, from her own verbal description of the robber—from the few short seconds she'd caught sight of his features.

"You're the only one who's seen Picasso without his mask," he added.

"Picasso?"

He shrugged. "That's what they call him. The guy's got a yen for expensive artwork. Never takes anything but pricey paintings. Likes to terrorize his victims too. Prefers to use a blade."

Martinique couldn't deny the truth of it. The creep had simply walked into her store during normal business hours, threatened her with the sharpest, most wicked-looking weapon she'd ever seen, and demanded the pictures on the wall. She'd been cool while it was happening, terrified and angry later.

Mimi, her shop assistant, had turned to mush, but Martinique had managed to hand over the merchandise without so much as a tremor. And then she'd watched helplessly as he'd sliced the paintings from their frames and rolled the canvases into a single, easy-to-carry tube.

Mimi had sobbed. Martinique had fumed silently. And the creep had gotten away.

"This guy has cost several antique art dealers some serious revenue," he told her. "The Dealer's Association wants him stopped. They want it bad enough to put up a very tempting pile of cash for whoever catches him. And in this case, I'm the whoever. With your help, that is, sweetness. You do remember the robbery, don't you?"

She remembered it, all right. She still felt sick inside just thinking about it. Not only for the loss of her paintings, which were worth plenty, but for what they'd represented. In the process of stealing those canvases, the crook had just as surely stolen her dreams.

She'd had plans for that money, plans she'd been making her entire life. The profit from those paintings had been earmarked for a down payment on a small house uptown. Not just any house, but a real *home*.

Where everything was clean and whitewashed, where there were flowers and sunshine and respectable families that went back for generations. Where the old guard of New Orleans lived. The society that Angelé had never been a part of.

But the robbery had put that dream on permanent hold. The police hadn't been able to trace the crook. And her low-cost insurance policy was turning out to be worthless. The idea that Cade Jackson might be able to make Picasso pay for his crime, and that he might even recover her paintings, was a pleasant one.

And there was the slim possibility that she could still identify him. Sure, he'd only been careless for an instant, when the elastic holding his purple plastic mask had slipped, revealing his face. But that instant had been long enough for her to remember what she saw.

Cruelty. Arrogance. Ugliness.

He had the look of a man who loved what he did for a living. A smile that said he took pleasure in inflicting pain.

She pushed the image to the back of her mind, almost wishing she *didn't* remember it. "Believe me, Mr. Jackson, I'd be happy to help. But you'll have to come back after business hours. Right now I need to get the shop open." There. It was a sensible solution to the problem. She was finally regaining control of the situation. She favored him with a calm, diplomatic smile. "And I'm sure you'd like some time to look after that wound? Clean up a little, maybe take a shower?"

She stood up, indicating that the conversation had come to an end. But Cade Jackson apparently didn't understand her polite signal. Either that, or he'd purposely decided to ignore it. He just sat there as comfortable as you please, studying her with that lazy, I'm-still-in-control-here look.

He raked back a wave of midnight hair from his eyes. "Still smell a little too ripe for a nice girl like you, do I? Kind of raw, not all sweet and squeaky clean?"

Before she'd had a chance to utter a single word, he eased himself out of the chair, strolled over to her fountain, and plunged his head and shoulders into the deep, gurgling water of the large concrete basin. Foaming liquid spilled over the side, sloshing onto the courtyard floor, bubbling up between the sun-warmed cracks like steam dancing off the Mississippi on a cool morning. He raised himself up again to his full six-foot height, flung his head back and let the water stream down around him.

Martinique's pulse picked up considerably as she noticed the change his instant bath had wrought. The blood and dirt were gone from his face, but that wasn't exactly what caught her attention.

It was the way his hair spilled back from his temples, wet, dripping, and sensual, cascading below his ears in a mass of sleek, gleaming blackness. It was the way the damp planes of his face looked like liquid on stone, as if an artist had lovingly chiseled the lines and angles into relief, then washed the dust away for the full, final impact. It was the way his shirt was plastered to his chest, leaving every bit of steel-forged sinew naked to her sight.

"Better, angel-face? Do I look more presentable now?"

Presentable? She wasn't sure how to describe him. It was hard to get beyond all that moist, muscled machismo. It was hard to pretend she didn't notice it. But his unpredictable behavior was even more disturbing. All her experience in the business world had never taught her how to deal with a man like this.

He was far too real for her taste. Too male. Too . . . much. "Fine," she managed, her mouth as dry as day-old beignets. "You look . . . fine."

He wrung some of the excess water from his hair. "Good. But before I leave, there's one little detail we need to discuss. Something about Picasso I forgot to mention."

"Oh? What's that? No, let me guess. He's an ax murderer on the side, right? Or maybe a serial rapist?"

Cade decided the lady had lots of cheek. Spunk and spice and sugar-laced sarcasm. Cade decided he kind of liked that about her. "Settle down, sweetheart. If the guy so much as touches you, he's dead meat. No one's going to lay a hand on you while I'm around."

No one but him, Cade swore silently. Martinique Duval was his responsibility at the moment. And she needed his protection much more than she realized.

"Now look here, Mr. Jackson—"

He gave her a slow once-over. "Sure thing, angel-face. Don't mind if I do."

"That's not what I meant! And don't call me that. Try Martinique if you can't manage the long version."

He liked the way her face had grown all warm and flushed beneath her skin. Like hot cream mixed with the fire of Caribbean rum. Like cognac laced with coffee and a dash of golden amaretto. What was it they called a drink like that? A Velvet Sin Stinger, straight up? A Sweet Maria Soother?

"Mar-tin-ique," she prompted. "Want me to spell it for you?"

"Martinique, huh? *Mar-tin-ique*," he repeated in a low, intimate voice, letting the word slide smoothly across his tongue. "Sorry, too formal for my taste. Guess I'll have to call you Nick instead. Nick Duval. Yeah, I think I like it. Nice and casual. Kinda loose."

"Nick?"

Cade couldn't help smiling to himself. He sort of enjoyed watching her get all worked up. Hot and feisty and ready to fight. Despite the proper, all-business exterior, she was pure determination inside. Like a solid steel cupcake with vanilla-cream frosting.

Nick. The name fit her. She was one tough Twinkie.

But as much as he liked to watch her, the most urgent need was to protect her. The recent bash to his head was a sure indication he might've brought her more trouble than he'd intended. Originally, he'd wanted only to question her. But now he needed more.

"Cool your jets." He ignored the look of indignant outrage that flashed across her wide green eyes. "It's time for the bad news."

How to tell her she might be in danger, that was the question. How to tell her he'd brought it on her himself.

The ugly boys down at the Boozery had admitted to seeing Picasso around. They'd confirmed Cade's suspicion that the perp was still in the area, but none of the gutless pea-brains had been willing to divulge his home address. Not that it would've done him much good. A clever crook like Picasso was smart enough to keep moving.

But judging by the gash on the back of his head, and the small black ink streak scribbled at the base of his arm, Cade knew he had to be hot on the trail, getting too close for comfort, in fact. Picasso had made that mark on him. Cade was sure of it. He'd seen it before in the police files, remembered that the pseudo-artistic little creep sometimes liked to sign his "work." In this case it was a clear warning. The signature meant *stay away*.

Some of the Boozery slimes must've tipped his hand. Picasso had known he was headed to the antique shop. He'd probably been waiting for him when he arrived.

It'd been stupid, a real no-brainer, but he'd let himself get distracted by a woman. Understandable, sure, especially with a woman like Nick. But not too bright. He'd broken rule number five from Jackson's Guide to Street Survival. *Never lose focus*.

Picasso had taken advantage of that one weak moment and nailed him, but good. Still, Cade didn't regret visiting the Boozery. Sometimes it was best to take the direct route.

Sometimes, if the perp knew he was being tracked, it'd shake him up and he'd start to get careless. Sometimes he'd be relieved and just give up so he could stop looking over his shoulder all the time. But he might as easily sneak up behind you and crack you over the head with a bottle of booze. That's what made the bounty-hunting business so interesting. You just never knew what was going to happen next.

But pretty soon now Picasso was going to figure out that a whiskey bottle to the brain was only a minor setback for a hard-headed bounty hunter. Pretty soon he'd figure out that Cade Jackson didn't give up so easily. He'd be watching Martinique's store, her home. And Cade needed to keep an eye out for him, to keep an eye out for *her*. He needed to stick around.

The direct route, that was how to break it to her. Rule number eight in the manual. *Keep it simple, stupid*.

"Picasso's already left me his calling card," he told her, indicating the back of his arm.

Martinique's eyes narrowed as she inspected the strange scribbled mark. "His what? What is that?"

"His John Hancock. A little sloppy, but no doubt the boy was in a big hurry."

Cade waited patiently while she took another look.

"He *signed* you? That's sick!"

Cade nodded with satisfaction. "Sure, but it's a good clue. Means his ego's bigger than his brain." He rubbed the back of his head. "Although he does have good aim. But at least we know where we stand. It's a safe bet he's going to pay us a return visit. To see how his artwork turned out."

"Us?" she asked, eyeing him warily.

"*Us*, Nick. He knows you can ID him. And now that he knows I'm after him, he'll come nosing around here to find out what happened. And I plan to be waiting for him when he does."

"Waiting . . ." Her eyes flashed and widened as the message started sinking in. "Oh, I don't think so, Jackson. Not unless you'd like to haul this blanket back to the gutter and camp out there."

"Actually, I had something more comfortable in mind. Your couch, for instance."

"No deal, buster. No *way*."

Cade studied the stubborn look in her eye and decided he liked the challenge. He'd always loved the thrill of the chase, and Nick was the kind who'd give him a good one. He wondered how long she'd be able to keep up the don't-you-dare-touch-me act. Days?

Weeks? With a woman wound up as tight as she was, it could take plenty of time. Probably more than he cared to expend in one place.

A good bounty hunter had to stay mobile to track his prey, always on the move. It was rule number two, *Never slow down*, and it was the only way to keep the trail clean and fresh. When he'd been younger, it had been an easy rule to follow. Now at thirty-five, he was simply afraid to stick around too long.

Some comfortable, cozy spot might lure a man in, make him soft. A man might never want to leave. And no matter what happened between Nick and him, he'd have to be moving on. Preferably sooner rather than later.

"Suit yourself, Nick. When Picasso shows up, tell him he can find me down at Killer's gym on the wharf. I'm outta here." He turned his back on her and headed for the gate.

"Outta here?" she called after him, disbelieving. "You mean that's it, and I'm supposed to face this creep alone? Why don't you go get him? What kind of bounty hunter are you, anyway?"

He glanced back in her direction. "An ornery one. I call the shots, or I don't do the job."

Martinique couldn't believe he was going to desert her, just like that. Or maybe she could. It was exactly what her childhood had led her to expect from men of his type. Men with no roots. Men you couldn't depend on. Except for one thing. You could always count on them to leave at the worst time.

There had been a string of them in Angelé's life,

including Martinique's own father. He'd taken off long before she'd been born. But she'd been reminded of him so many times—growing up, struggling through school.

The sorority girls at college had been the cruelest. They'd wanted nothing to do with a low-class scholarship recipient who'd had no money, and worse, no decent family background. Martinique's daddy didn't have a prominent position in the community. In fact, her mother didn't even know her daddy's name. She knew only that he was one of many men who'd sampled Angelé's talents some twenty-eight years ago.

On weekends the sorority girls had gone to debutante balls dressed in long white gowns, their wrists perfumed with flowers, their waists encircled by the willing arms of eligible young men. Martinique had gone home to the small apartment she'd grown up in, wiped the dried-up vomit from her mother's face, and tried to shut out the stench and noise of the bar-filled street below.

Men had stopped coming to the apartment long ago, and the aging Angelé had turned to liquor for comfort instead. Two months before Martinique's graduation, she'd finally drunk herself to death.

And Martinique, alone, had continued to look after herself in the same careful, grown-up way she always had. The same way she intended to now.

"Look, Jackson, be reasonable. You *can't* stay here. We don't even know each other!"

"Yeah," he said, his face relaxing into a slow, speculative smile. "What a waste. It could've been interesting."

Interesting? Martinique wondered silently. Risky

was a lot more like it. "There's a quaint little hotel just around the corner," she suggested hopefully. "I could make you a reservation and—"

"No deal," he shot back, cutting her off. "Either I'm here or I'm history."

"Some option," she murmured in frustration. It was a simple, no-win situation. Jackson or Picasso. Conan or the creep.

Both men were dangerous, but in decidedly different ways. Picasso was a threat to her livelihood, her safety. Jackson was a threat to her . . . Lord, she didn't even want to think about that. But anything was better than being held up again, maybe even being hurt this time.

"You can camp out in the courtyard," she told him firmly. "But you'll have to wash up somewhere else. Down at Killer's gym, for instance." There. That sounded decisive, businesslike. It was impersonal. It let him know where he stood.

He raised those dark eyebrows at her, questioning, but she held her ground, folding her arms across her chest and matching him stare for stare. "It's my best offer," she said smoothly. "Take it or leave it."

"I'll take it," he told her, with just a hint of a smile playing at the stubble-roughened edges of his mouth. "For now."

THREE

Cade cranked the gears on his motorcycle up to full throttle, pushing the limits of the chrome-covered engine until it whined and throbbed, responding beneath him with a fierce surge of speed. He leaned forward in the leather seat and coaxed the last ounce of quivering velocity from the straining machine as it rocketed smoothly down the long stretch of street. He let the wind buffet him, felt the shuddering rush of air all the way down to his soul.

Acceleration and high-performance horsepower. Stainless steel satisfaction. They still had the potency to bring him pleasure as so few things did anymore.

After twelve years on the road, twelve years on the rough edge of life, he was no longer a naive kid with the world by the tail. He was beat-up, burned-out, and kicks were a lot harder to come by these days.

After years of pursuing reluctant perps, his body had been banged up pretty bad. He'd been stomped, stabbed, punched, kicked, shot at and missed, shot at and hit, and whacked on the head with everything from beer mugs to pool cues. But he wasn't numb, yet.

The pulse of pure speed in his hands, the mastery of the sleek, screaming machine—that still felt good, still stirred him like red-hot Cajun cooking, burning him down to the core.

Women, too, were just as interesting as ever. Women like Nick, anyway. In fact, he hadn't laid eyes on anything quite so fascinating in a long time. Nick Duval, the dark-haired seductress in debutante disguise. If she ever let him near enough, he bet she'd take him on the ride of a lifetime.

He took the final curve to the back of Killer's gym, whipped the bike into the gravel lot, and parked it with an easy snap to the kickstand. Inside, he headed for the locker room, dropped his duffel bag on the nearest wooden bench, and started to strip.

Killer's wasn't much of a gym by most standards. No high-tech equipment, no plastic membership cards, no full-length mirrors or perky women in tight spandex suits. Just a single locker room with showers and an old warehouse full of iron weights. Just a place where a man could clear his head and let his body master the pain.

In shorts and leather half-gloves, he approached the bench press, rolled onto his back, and gripped the chest bar with both hands. With a single flex of his straining biceps, he willed the weights upward. Mind over matter, he told himself, exhaling hard. Clear the brain and welcome the pain.

A few more extensions of the bar and the pain was

starting to register in his body. He could feel it coursing through him, pumping into his veins like heavy molten lead and hot battery acid. But his mind couldn't completely control it this time. He was distracted again, dammit. By *her*.

He wondered if she really could help lead him to Picasso, if she might have a clue the police didn't pick up in their report. He knew from experience, from his first fast-lane year as a rookie cop, that every bit of vital information didn't always make it into the report. Paperwork wasn't always high on the list of police priorities.

The sweat was starting to sheen across his bare body now, the torture in his muscles was becoming even more intense, but he cracked a quick smile, remembering how Rand, his rookie partner and lifelong buddy, had been so bad at taking notes. But then, neither of them had been whizzes at school. They'd been far too busy with more important boyhood activities.

Essential stuff, like long lazy days spent fishing in the bayou and scouting through the cypress, hunting for swamp monsters. And when they were older, wild weekends racing dirt bikes, churning up speedboat waves for the tourist paddlewheelers along the Mississippi, sneaking that first illicit taste of beer together, and cruising the gravel-paved streets of their tiny Cajun hometown, chasing skirts.

No, Rand hadn't been much of a scholar, but he'd sure been a helluva friend.

Cade's gut was starting to burn now, the perspiration beading on his forehead as he grunted out the second set of lifts, the weights wrenching at his stomach muscles as the memories tugged at his mind. He could still recall standing up as best man at Rand's wedding, amazed that Lori had finally tamed him, and a little jealous. Rand had a wife, a house, someone to go home to. Cade had no one. His folks had divorced and written him off as a loser long ago.

But the marriage thing had turned out better than he'd expected. The newlyweds had treated him like family, and Lori had become the little sister he'd never had. Cade had liked to hang out at their house on weekends, just to kick back and enjoy the peace. And he and Rand had still been the roughest, toughest rookies on the whole Acadiana police force. Unstoppable. Invincible.

Until the night that Rand had been killed by a single bullet, fired from the gun of a dirt-licking cockroach they'd busted just the week before. A scumbag who was out on bail, high on drugs, and wanted a little payback.

Cade felt the blood beating in his ears now, pumping through him hot and angry, his body sweat-lathered and drenched in wet, steaming agony. He gave in to the pain, let it take him. He *was* the pain.

But the memories always ripped at him most of all. He was never free of them, no matter how far he tried to run. A week after Rand's funeral he'd hit the road and never looked back. He'd taken care of Rand's killer first, tracked him down and sent him to jail forever. But the satisfaction had been small, fleeting, and bittersweet. And it had left him with an even more insatiable taste for revenge.

He'd started hunting for bounty full-time. The loss had left him anesthetized, unafraid to take risks. And his reckless reputation had spread. Cowboy Jackson, they said, was half crazed. One hand short of a full deck. A dude with a death wish.

He laughed softly, realizing that the ache in his body was nothing now. He *liked* the pain in his muscles. It helped him forget about the ache inside.

Locking the weights down into the metal rest, he eased himself out from under them and stood to work the punching bag. He had to prepare himself mentally, physically. There was another chase ahead. Another challenge to live or die for and no one to leave behind. No one to miss him. Not a single bloody soul.

But the hunt was everything. The stink of the crook ahead, the rancid trail, and at the end, the heart-pounding reward as he moved in for the kill.

Winding his fists up tight, he pummeled the hard-packed material, beating it relentlessly into submission. It was just the kind of release he craved. The kind of release he got when he turned the in latest perp for the prize.

He didn't track them for the money, although after all these years he did have a hefty nest egg stashed away. No, he did it because he *needed* to. It was a profession with no medical benefits but plenty of job satisfaction.

A profession where a single distraction could be fatal.

And it scared the hell out of him, he who was seldom afraid of anything, to realize that a distraction like Martinique Duval might be worth the risk.

———◆———◆———

"Sweet potato pralines! Now, that's what I call a customer!"

Martinique glanced up from her daily ledger to see exactly who or what her outspoken shop assistant had found so fascinating. One look out the front window told her it was definitely a who. A who on a Harley.

She willed her gaze back to the ledger and her voice took on a tone of practiced, professional nonchalance. "He's not a customer, Mimi. He's here to— He's here on business."

As if to contradict her careful words, the bike let out a final rumbling roar, about two decibels below a foghorn. God, she might've guessed that Cade Jackson would ride a motorcycle. The ugliest, most awesome chrome-infested steel monster she'd ever seen. All that surging speed and pent-up power suited him perfectly. He looked like some dark knight on the back of a modern metal dragon with its charred black tailpipe spitting fire and smoke.

Mimi let out a low, flirtatious wolf-whistle. "I'd like to do a little business with that one myself. Only I wouldn't charge him a dime."

Martinique tried to look shocked, but she knew Mimi's past too well for that. Her barely twenty-year-old assistant had been an inexperienced, incredibly naive streetwalker nicknamed Mimosa only six months before. Mimosa, fresh out of school with no place to go, sweet and bubbly and scared.

Always a sucker for a hard-luck case, Martinique had

hired her for the shop and given her a chance at a new life. And with a little training, Mimi had worked out just fine. Until now. One look at Cade Jackson and the girl was regressing like crazy.

"Quit gawking, Mimi. He's just a man."

"He certainly is," Mimi said with a sigh.

Martinique couldn't quite explain the irritation she felt. She'd wanted Mimi to maintain a little dignity, but the girl had a wild streak that couldn't be rubbed out. Maybe the tendency to transgress really was in the genes after all. Maybe she'd been drawn to the girl because she knew the same thing might just as easily have happened to her.

Martinique looked up again as the little bell over the door chimed softly and Cade's heavy leather boots echoed across the marble threshold of her shop.

"Evening, Nick."

Martinique tried not to stare, but she couldn't help noticing the difference that a little soap and water had made. Gone were the dirty, dripping hair, the blood-stained scalp, the raunchy smell. The man in front of her was still cocky, raw, and sporting blue jeans, but basically, a nice girl's nightmare. Swaggering, reckless, and sexier than sin.

Definitely *not* her type at all.

Closing the account book, Martinique stood up. "Mr. Jackson. I'd like to introduce you to Mimi, my assistant."

"Pleasure," he said, treating the girl to one of his trademark smiles.

Mimi looked as though she was about to giggle.

Martinique glanced impatiently at the gilt clock over the fireplace mantle. "It's nearly closing time, Mimi. Take off now, if you'd like. I can handle it from here."

But when her fascinated assistant reluctantly closed the door behind her, Martinique wondered if she really could handle Jackson alone. This morning he'd been hurting, a little weak from the blow to his head. But even the memory of it seemed ridiculous now. Cade Jackson weak? He was power on the prowl. Sheer energy, unleashed.

And in the open air of the courtyard, he hadn't looked so *large*. So blatantly masculine. In the tiny confines of her shop, he towered over the delicate French furniture and antique accessories, throwing her carefully planned ambience into visual chaos. With a specimen like that in the room, so overpowering, so recherché, it was impossible to notice anything else.

He sank down onto the silk Aubusson sofa, stretched his booted legs across the Persian carpet, and made himself at home. "Relax, Nick. I'm going to."

She crossed her arms over her chest and gave him a defensive glare. "I'm perfectly relaxed."

"Uh-huh." He produced a brown paper sack from the depths of his shining black motorcycle helmet and tossed it onto her coffee table. "This oughta loosen you up a little."

She eyed the sack suspiciously. "What is it? No, let me guess. Mad Dawg malt liquor? A Big Swig in a bag?"

He let out a low, rusty laugh. "Not even close. It's dinner. Not exactly the way I wanted to show my appreciation, but I can't let a lady save my life without at least bringing her some carryout, now can I?"

He dumped the contents onto the table: two sealed styrofoam containers, a few napkins, and a pair of plastic forks. A sharp scent wafted up to Martinique's nostrils, redolent of rich, dark spices and bold tropical seasonings. She took a few cautious steps toward the food. "Thanks," she murmured doubtfully. "I think."

Cade reached up and caught her by the wrist. "It's not fried gator, sweetness. It won't bite you. And neither will I."

Martinique didn't even bother to resist when he gave her arm a quick tug and pulled her down beside him on the sofa.

"Now, eat up, Nick. You're gonna love this." He dipped up a forkful of something steamy and strange looking and, when she opened her lips to protest, popped it into her mouth.

Martinique's eyes widened in surprise, but as soon as she started chewing, she knew she liked it. The flavor was unusual, strong but deliciously laced with powerful spices. *Hot* spices. By the time she'd swallowed, her mouth was on fire.

"Water—" she croaked.

He handed her a leather drinking pouch from his pocket, the kind that desert Bedouins carried on the backs of their camels. Martinique didn't bother to ask what it was. At this point anything wet and liquid would do. She tilted her head back and gulped down half the contents.

And immediately realized that it wasn't water. Her

mouth wasn't burning anymore, but the drink he'd given her, whatever it was, was scorching an eighty-proof path all the way to her stomach.

She handed him back the pouch and, after a few deep breaths, shot him a hostile glare. "Are you trying to kill me?"

He shook his head. "Nope, I need you alive. And if you're worried I might be trying to get you drunk and take advantage, you're wrong there too. If I ever did seduce you, sweetness, I'd rather have you wide awake, so you can tell me what you want and I can see the pleasure on your face when I give it to you."

It took a moment for his words to register in her brain and another ten seconds for the hot, full-body flush to work its way clear down to her toes. She couldn't believe he'd said those things to her. She couldn't believe she'd let him.

So here was her cue to stand up, slap his face, and tell him to hit the road, Jackson. Here was the time to hand him his walking papers. Instead she grabbed the pouch out of his hand, took another swallow, and eyed him defiantly. "This is a business relationship, Mr. Jackson. I'd be pleased if you remember that."

He shrugged, took a bite of the hot dish from hell, and continued to watch her. "Whatever you say. But you might be more pleased if I didn't."

Thoroughly rattled, Martinique picked up her own fork and shoveled in a second mouthful of the stuff. Surprisingly, it went down a lot easier this time. An effect of the alcohol, she figured. Her mouth was proba-

bly still on fire, but she was just too intoxicated to realize it.

They finished dinner in silence, and when the sky
outside turned dark and hazy with purple mist, Martinique locked the front door and lit the large clusters of
candles in their antique sconces. She spotted the half-
full decanter of wine by her desk, the one normally re-
served for her customers, and knew it was just what she
needed to wash the unfamiliar tastes from her mouth.
Another swig of that pouch concoction and she'd be the
one sleeping it off in the street. She uncorked the bottle,
filled two crystal goblets with the amber liquid, and
handed one to Cade.

"So, what do you call that dish anyway?" she asked
him. "Just so I can remember what not to order next
time."

He settled back on the sofa and propped his legs on
the carved wooden coffee table. Martinique didn't
mind. She sat down on a prim opera chair, across from
the couch, and watched him.

There was something fascinating about the contrast.
The ornate, luxuriously gilded tabletop supporting
those long legs shod in rough, rawhide leather boots.
The coarseness of his jeans against the fine silk of the
sofa. The pale, intricate tapestry silhouetting his steel-
corded arms and sinewed shoulders. The satin brocade
pillows painted with the dark streaks of his hair.

He wasn't uncomfortable around the luxury. He let
it accommodate him, used it to his liking.

His fingers curled casually, powerfully around the
stem of the delicate glass goblet, the wine glowing red-

gold in the candlelight. Martinique stared at the goblet, at the fingers that held it, and swallowed hard.

"It's a Cajun recipe," he explained, "the Slow Burn Special, from a little joint I know. Guess it's an acquired taste. I grew up in a little bayou burg around Acadiana."

A Cajun kid, Martinique mused. She might've known. They were a tough, independent breed who'd settled the swampy land along the Teche long before the American government was born. Where the living was hard and fast and only the strong survived. And Cade was clearly one of their descendants. She could see it in his bold blue eyes, in the sensuality of his hard-edged, faintly French features, in the dense velvet darkness of his hair.

She could hear it in the deep, exotic strength of his voice. There was an earthy, ancient Gallic accent there she hadn't quite defined before.

"So, where you from, Nick? One of those muckety-muck mansions uptown, right?"

She shook her head, smiling softly. "Not quite. But growing up, I always wished that I did live there. It looked so—happy. The little girls in those houses slept in canopy beds, and their mothers tucked them in at night and read them bedtime stories." She felt a lump rising in her throat, but tamped it down, still smiling. "At least that's how I imagined it."

He tossed back another sip of wine and studied her thoughtfully. "It's good to have dreams, as long as you don't give up on them. It doesn't hurt until you quit fighting for what you want."

She wondered suddenly if he understood the subject

theoretically or from personal experience. What had Cowboy Cade ever dreamed of? An engraved plaque in the Hell's Angels' hall of fame? A lifetime subscription to *Mercenary Magazine*?

As for her dreams, well, at least some of them had come true.

The professional ones, anyway. Her latest coup was an appointment to the board of the art museum. Serving there had been a goal ever since she'd graduated from Sophie Newcomb College with an art history degree. The museum director had admired her "exquisite" shop and deemed her taste and education perfect for the position.

And suddenly those same sorority sisters who had ignored her years ago were inviting her to their uptown mansions for decorating advice. And their slightly bored husbands often made invitations of a different kind. Martinique usually sold the women her costliest antiques, but she always declined the men. She might be a Duval woman, the type men never seemed to marry, but Martinique vowed she would not be any man's mistress.

It was almost laughable, since she was now considered so exotic, so worldly and sophisticated. But it was true. The chic owner of Heirloom Antiques had never let a man get close enough to touch her.

She could count the number of dates she'd had on one hand. They'd been little more than groping matches with hormone-happy college boys. But Martinique knew exactly what would happen if you let a man go too far. She'd seen it happen to her mother a hundred times. Most of Angelé's "dates" were gone the next day. The loyal ones would stay for a week or two, but when they finally walked out, Angelé had suffered even more.

Those years had been tough, but they'd taught Martinique the most important lesson of her life. It was a bad idea to go to bed with a man, but it was fatal to fall in love.

So she'd sworn herself to safe, comfortable celibacy. She'd sworn never to let a man in her life unless he intended to stay for good. Forever.

She was still holding out for someone nice and stable to come along. Some tweedy professor type—a safe, stay-at-home gentleman who'd keep her company on long, lonely weekends. Someone respectable and faithful. Someone who wouldn't leave.

"I still have a dream or two left," she said. "Only the biggest one belongs to Picasso right now. Those paintings he took were the most valuable pieces in my shop. The money they were going to bring was going to go toward a small house uptown. Not one of those big mansions. Just something average-sized I could've called my own."

Cade shot a speculative look around the shop. "Seems like a pretty good place you've got here. Don't lots of people want to live in the Quarter?"

She nodded. "I guess they do. But I'm just renting the space right now. And I want something different. Someplace I can put down roots. A real home."

"The picket fence thing," he said, nodding. "I'm kinda surprised, Nick. You seem to fit in here so well.

All plush and elegant. I never would've guessed you had a longing for suburbia."

She'd bet there were a few other things he'd never guess about her, either. "Maybe I'll surprise you again," she suggested defensively. "Maybe I'll fit in there just as well."

"I meant it as a compliment," he told her. "I'm sure you'd do just fine living anywhere you damn well please. But let me guess. Is there a husband in the scenario somewhere? Maybe a docile, good-old-dog type to share the space with?"

She gave him a cool glare, secretly irritated that he'd been able to read her so easily. "Not yet. But someday, yes, I probably will get married to a nice guy. Anything wrong with that?"

"Nothing at all," he told her. "If you're sure that's really what you want."

She didn't answer. She wasn't sure what to say.

He reached across the narrow table and gave a gentle tug on her hair. "Admit it, Nick. It's going to take a lot more man than that to keep a lady like you interested."

She felt his callused fingertips brush against her throat and pulled back, her heart beating wildly. "I don't know what you're talking about."

He leaned closer, close enough to kiss her. "Want me to demonstrate?"

Yes, she whispered silently. But since when did any of the Duval women want what was good for them? She stood abruptly, backing away. "What I want is to help you find Picasso."

He leaned back, tossing off the last of his wine. "Anything you say. And I promise you we will find him. And then you can have that little house you're after and I can be on my way. Meanwhile, we have to locate ourselves an art fence. Happen to know any in town?"

"Dozens," she responded sarcastically. "Many of my customers actually prefer stolen merchandise. It lends any object a certain cachet, no?"

"Think hard, Nick. You must be well connected in the business. Where can we ask around?"

She did think hard. And the best opportunity that came to mind was the upcoming party at the art museum. But she seriously doubted if Jackson had ever worn a tuxedo in his life. Did they even make them for men with shoulders that size?

"Earth to Nick."

"Well, there is a fund-raiser this weekend at the art museum. Everybody who's anybody in the business will be there. Buyers and sellers both."

"Bingo. Sign us up."

She hesitated, biting softly on her lower lip. "But it's formal. . . ."

"What, no topless mud wrestling?" he asked, looking disappointed.

She rolled her eyes, studying him skeptically. "Do you even know how to dance?"

He cocked his head to one side. "Lady, besides bounty hunting, there's only one thing I do really well. And it's a lot like dancing."

Martinique felt her toes curling inside her shoes. Folding her arms across her chest, she tried to keep her voice steady. "Right. I'm sure the women of the world whisper prayers of thanks into their pillows every night. Except I'm talking about *dancing* here, bub. The waltz, the fox-trot, that kind of stuff."

He stood, wrapped one arm around her waist, and pulled her to him. "Guess you'll have to show me."

Martinique would have tried to move if she hadn't been taken so completely by surprise. But apparently Cade didn't think it was any big deal going pelvis-to-pelvis with someone he'd just met that morning.

And as if that weren't bold and brazen enough, his hips were starting to grind audaciously against hers, slowly, rhythmically moving to the beat of some imaginary Latin sound. And just as inexorably, her own body was starting to respond.

Her stomach squeezed and tightened as he pushed closer, rocking her from side to side with the silent sway of the music. She started to pull away, then sank into him, reveling in the heady feel of it. Bare muscle against smooth skin. Male against female. Hard against soft.

"Way to go, Nick." He bent his head close to whisper in her ear. "I knew you had it in you. Real talent."

Martinique froze at the words. *Real talent.* Exactly what Angelé had had, according to a large percentage of the city's male population. A real knack for balancing on a two-foot-wide tabletop and taking her clothes off one piece at a time.

She wrenched herself free, out of his reach. "Sorry, Jackson, but you've got the wrong lady. I'm not just another notch for your holster, *comprendez-vous?* The lesson's over. Time to sack out in the courtyard the way we agreed."

He didn't move, just hooked his thumbs in the side pockets of his blue jeans and studied her thoughtfully. "Afraid, angel-face?"

"Afraid? Ha! Try intelligent, Jackson. Try careful, cautious, and coolheaded."

He gave her a wry grin. "I was."

By midnight Martinique still hadn't slept. At ten o'clock she'd worried about Cade camping out in the courtyard with a cold fog rolling in from the east. After all, he'd been injured, hadn't he? The weather might make him worse, maybe even kill him, and then how would she ever get her paintings back? At eleven she'd unlocked the front door, called down from her window, and offered him the spare bedroom. It was the least she could do.

But ever since she'd heard his hard boots creaking up the old wooden stairs and known he was in the house, she hadn't been able to relax. Ming and Ching had been dozing on her bedroom chaise for hours. The street noise had died down long ago. And she was probably the only living creature still awake on her whole block. At least that was how it felt.

Until she heard the noise.

It was a faint bump, maybe a squirrel or a cat leaping on or off her balcony outside. Or maybe it was Picasso, coming back to pay her a second visit. She sat up in bed, her heart pounding.

A second bump had her scrambling down the narrow hallway and fumbling with the polished glass knob on Jackson's door. She was inside the room before she had sufficient time to think. And instantly regretted the decision.

He was still asleep, thank goodness. Sprawled out on his stomach, his long legs dwarfing the fragile footboard, one arm strangling a large down pillow, a thick wave of black hair curling across his forehead. The bedclothes had been kicked away, bunched into a crumpled pile at his feet.

And there wasn't another scrap of fabric anywhere in sight.

Nada. Nothing. Zippo. The man was naked, for heaven's sake.

Martinique gulped air, grateful that she'd found him lying on his belly instead of his back. A sight like that could send the world's oldest living virgin right over the edge.

Uncertain whether to stay or flee straight back to her bedroom, she heard the bump again. That settled it. She took a few steps toward the bed, caught hold of the sheet, and started to draw it up over him.

And got the shock of her life. The arm that had been holding the pillow reached out for her instead, pulling her off balance and down onto the bed beside him.

"Mmmm . . ." he mumbled, half asleep, as his other arm stole around her waist, locking her close. His fingers began a playful, teasing exploration across the soft mound of her breast.

Martinique froze, her heart pumping furiously. But the fingers kept moving, back and forth, cupping and stroking the rosy tip until it peaked and tautened with pleasure. She couldn't breathe. She didn't dare. The sensation was so sweet, she had to bite her tongue to keep from whimpering.

When he made a move to bring his other hand into play, she couldn't take it anymore and finally managed a weak "What are you *doing*?"

Instantly he seemed to come fully awake. Two seconds later Martinique found herself flat on her back beneath him, her arms pinned over her head, her legs locked tightly between his. And at her throat she felt the rigid barrel of a gun, heard the chilling click of the hammer being cocked.

How lucky for her that Jackson was ready to shoot intruders at a moment's notice. And how unfortunate that he'd mistaken her for one of them. He stared down at her, looking dazed and disoriented yet ready for battle.

And then she watched realization dawn in his heavy, hooded blue eyes. He disarmed the weapon, dropped it onto the nightstand, and smiled with satisfaction. His gaze roved over the flimsy lace of her nightgown, the creamy rise and fall of her breasts, the dark, swollen centers. His voice was hoarse when he spoke, thick with interest and approval. "Changed your mind, have you, Nick?"

Before she had a chance to respond, his mouth came

down over hers, subduing her into silence. And suddenly all thoughts of speech or resistance or noises in the night vanished from Martinique's brain as he took her to a place she'd never been before, mastering her with a slow, melting, mind-blowing kiss.

FOUR

Martinique's mouth opened, not in protest, but in pure passionate response to Cade's kiss. She felt his tongue slip inside, touching, tasting, exploring with a shameless intimacy that should've shocked her. It didn't.

It made her melt. It made her wet and crazy and weak with pleasure. It left her wanting more.

And all at once she wasn't afraid to show it. Something snapped inside. Her inhibitions fled.

She kissed him back.

Her body arched beneath him and she met his movements with her own, opening her arms, her legs, her mouth. She wanted to take him in more fully. She wanted to feel the length of him above her, to tangle her hands in his sleep-ruffled hair, to breathe in the rich male scent of him, dark and sweet, potent as midnight perfume.

Cade groaned and his voice echoed rusty and erotic

in her ear. "Lord, Nick, do you have any idea what you're doing to me?"

Martinique froze at the words, her body growing rigid with doubt and embarrassment as realization overcame her. Actually, she didn't have any idea what she was doing at all. She'd never behaved so brazenly before in her life. She'd never responded to a man so wildly, so wantonly.

She'd never forgive herself.

Cade let out a slow, ragged sigh, swearing softly. "Hell, sweet thing, I didn't mean for you to stop. You can do anything you want to me. Go ahead, torture me to death. I can't think of a better way to die."

He lowered his head to kiss her again, more carefully this time, but Martinique didn't move. She couldn't. "It was a mistake," she whispered, just before his mouth made contact again. "A misunderstanding."

Cade rolled over onto his back, releasing his hold on her. He dragged the sheet up to his waist, almost as an afterthought, as though his nakedness wasn't much matter for concern. "A misunderstanding? It sure didn't seem that way to me, angel-face. I thought we understood each other pretty well."

She was grateful for the cloak of darkness, grateful that he couldn't fully read her flushed, burning face. "I heard a noise," she explained, glancing nervously toward the window and the balcony beyond. "I only came in here for . . . protection."

It was the truth, after all. She'd simply been frightened. She'd only wanted to put Cade on the alert. She just hadn't realized that what awaited her in her own guest bedroom might be more disturbing than the danger that lurked outside.

Cade sat up in bed as soon as Nick's words sank in. She'd heard something outside. Might be nothing. Might be Picasso. But either way, it was clear she hadn't come for him.

Too bad. Hell, it was downright disappointing. But what had just happened between them was more than wishful thinking on his part. Whatever Nick's original intentions were, her reaction to his kiss had been real.

Real nice.

He'd never known a woman to explode in his arms so quickly, so completely. She'd been crazy with need, touching him everywhere, catching him completely off guard. Not that he'd minded. In fact, it was hard to remember the last time a single kiss had rocked him so hard. Especially one where the lady involved was still wearing some of her clothes.

He just hadn't dreamed that his prim, innocent Angel-face would be such a sensual seductress in bed. The turbulent passion locked inside her had taken him by surprise. And nothing surprised Cade Jackson.

Judging by Nick's sudden about-face in behavior, he was pretty sure it had shocked her too. Despite the sweet wildness she'd shown, it was clearly out of character for a lady like Ms. Duval to reveal that side of herself. Especially to a man like him.

She didn't have to say it out loud. He could read it in her body language. She was horrified by what had happened.

But that was her problem, wasn't it? It was time to

remember why he was there, to remind himself exactly what he was after.

Picasso. The crook. He pushed himself up from the bed and strode to the edge of the window, gun in hand. It was the chase he needed, not her.

He parted the lace-edged curtain with the barrel of his weapon and scanned the blackness beyond. "What did it sound like?"

"Just a short thump outside. No, two thumps. Maybe it was nothing."

"Maybe. But I'd better check the rest of the apartment, just to be sure." With his back still to her, he dropped the sheet on the floor and reached for yesterday's Levi's. "We can start with your bedroom," he said, easing himself into the jeans. He hoped the action was as uncomfortable for her to watch as it was for him to perform.

"Right."

He didn't miss the tension in her tone. There was some very perverse part of him that actually enjoyed it. Almost as much as he enjoyed invading the sanctity of her bedroom.

It was pretty much what he'd expected. A high ceiling, lots of creamy lace, and fancy floral wallpaper. Everything nice and neat and perfectly in place, except for the sheets on the bed. They were thrown back across the pale green bedcovers. Satin sheets.

Cade wondered if they helped her stay cool on hot New Orleans nights or if she liked the feel of them against her skin. He wondered what it would be like to lay her down against them and make love until the silky fabric was sheened with the perspiration from their bodies.

He wondered what the devil was wrong with him.

He wouldn't be hanging around long enough for anything like that to happen. Not with a lady like Nick, anyway. In spite of the passion he'd glimpsed within her, he knew she wasn't the kind of woman who'd want a short-term relationship, no matter how righteously good it promised to be.

No, Nick was the type who expected, and deserved, the big C. Commitment. Unfortunately, he just wasn't the type to give it.

He checked out the latch on the window to make sure it was locked, but mostly just for something to do. If anyone had been there before, they were probably long gone by now. Not much chance of nailing any crooks tonight.

"Try to get some sleep," he suggested. "I'll keep watch until it gets light." After the night moves with Nick, he'd be wide awake anyway.

Martinique nodded, carefully closing the door behind him. She felt less like sleeping than ever, so instead of slipping back between the covers, she curled up on the chaise, snuggling herself between Ming and Ching. There was something so comforting about a pair of warm, purring cats. They were such calm, peaceful creatures. They didn't go all crazy and unpredictable if you disturbed them in their sleep.

The way Cade had.

Or maybe what had happened was her fault. She wasn't very experienced with men. Especially men who

were completely naked and only half awake. She hadn't
realized how he would react to her. She hadn't realized
how she would react to him. She hadn't realized how
complicated life could become in the course of a single
day.

"I'm not sure this is such a good idea."

Martinique shook her head slowly and continued to
stare at the man in front of her. Cade, the blue-jean
bounty hunter, wore sleek black tuxedo pants, satin racing stripes down the sides, and a custom-pressed dress
shirt, open to the waist, its edges sharp as saber blades.
He'd already strapped a leather body holster over the
white shirt fabric and under his arms. The steel blue
sidearm lying low against his left side wouldn't be seen
beneath his jacket.

He looked devastating. Dressed to kill. The only
problem was, they were going to the museum fund-
raiser. She wondered what the other board members
would say if they discovered her "date" was packing a
weapon.

"Sure it is, Nick. We're gonna make out just fine
tonight. Now, give me a hand with these shirt studs,
would you?" He dropped a pile of them onto her open
palm and sank down beside her on the living room
couch, waiting.

Martinique let out a long sigh, leaned over, and
started threading the studs through his heavily starched
buttonholes. The task seemed simple enough, but it was

tough not to be distracted. God, but he smelled good. She couldn't seem to keep her hands from shaking.

"You look . . . different in a tux," she said, trying to keep her voice level and light. The statement didn't begin to do him justice. He looked more comfortable in formal clothes than she'd ever imagined. Cowboy Cade, it seemed, cleaned up pretty good.

She kept talking, hoping her fascination wasn't as obvious and ridiculously adolescent as it felt. "I mean, you've been here for three days and I don't think I've seen you in anything but blue jeans."

"Haven't you? Guess I remember it differently. . . ."

Martinique felt her face growing warm. "I wasn't talking about *that*. That doesn't count."

He gave her an understanding smile. "If you say so."

"I just meant, well, I imagine a man like you prefers to live—casually."

He laughed and the sound was surprisingly harsh. "A man like me? What a polite way to put it. But you're basically right. I don't dress to impress. The last time I went formal was for a friend's funeral. I sleep in the raw. I live on the road. And I like it that way."

She snapped the last stud in place and hesitated, scanning his expression. "But haven't you ever wanted something more permanent? Something with stability?"

"Stability? You mean a shirt and a tie and an employee pension plan? No thanks, sweetheart. Not for me. You think it looks nice, don't you? Well, let me tell you, sometimes the bad guys are the ones wearing the starched suits. Your knight in shining armor may show up one day dressed in black leather. So how are you going to tell them apart?"

She shook her head. "I don't know. I'm not looking for a knight. Tonight I'd be happy just to locate Picasso."

He nodded. "By the way, angel-face, did I tell you you look beautiful in that dress? You do, you know."

"I— Thank you."

She'd been a little disappointed he hadn't noticed it earlier. She'd purchased it the week before at the Canal Street mall, and the saleswoman had assured her it was just perfect for the occasion.

The simple gown of pale cream silk set off her dark hair nicely and made a smooth, straight line from the top of her neck all the way down to her ankles. No skin was showing except for what was revealed by a small slit up to the mid-calf, which made the dress easier to walk in. Nothing slinky. It was understatement all the way. Her favorite kind of outfit.

She hadn't expected a man like Cade to understand. He didn't.

"There's just one small thing that's bothering me about it." He pulled her off the couch and stepped back to better examine the outfit.

She blinked in disbelief. "Bothering you? Oh great. Just what I need. Fashion advice from Conan of the French Quarter. Or whatever it is they call you."

He scratched his chin slowly with one hand, then put two fingers across his lips, demanding her silence. "Don't worry, I think I know what it is."

"I wasn't worried. I was wondering if I could get in a quick punch before you pulled that gun on me again."

"Probably not. Be nice, Nick."

"Nice? That's some suggestion, coming from a man who doesn't have the decency to at least pretend he likes a lady's dress."

"Sorry. I don't usually do the decent thing."

As if to back up his words with action, he leaned over, rolled up the cuff of his left pant leg, and withdrew something sharp and shiny. Martinique didn't react immediately. She was too fascinated by the leather knife sheath strapped around his ankle to do anything but stare.

Cade knelt in front of her. There was a flash of steel, a quick upward slash, and the job was done. In one deft, daring movement, he'd turned her short, sensible walking slit into a risqué rift that ran halfway up her thigh.

She heard herself gasp. "I—I can't believe you did that!"

He calmly sheathed the knife again and rolled the black leg of his pants back down. "Believe it, babe."

"Why?" she whispered, still staring at her naked leg in shock.

"Because you needed it, Nick. Because I wanted to. Because we're going to shake them up tonight."

She looked up and let out a short, breathless laugh. "You're off the deep end, aren't you? Looney. Bonkers. Bananas. One of those people who loves to take risks, just for the thrill of it, am I right? You're *dangerous*."

He gave her an appreciative stare, taking in the full length of her, letting his gaze slide up leisurely, lazily, a little at a time. Martinique's knees nearly buckled beneath her. When Cade's eyes finally met hers, they were steel blue, sympathetic, and sizzling with desire.

"You're right, darlin'," he said softly. "I am crazy. But you're the one who's dangerous."

Martinique felt her stomach squeeze tight. She looked away, trying to break the tension. "You don't understand. I can't go looking like this. It's too—"

"Sexy?"

"Revealing. It's just not the kind of dress I'd normally wear."

"I do understand, Nick. You're scared. Not because the dress feels wrong. You're afraid because it feels too right."

She shook her head, ready to deny it, then stopped, wondering if there was any truth in what he'd said. She wasn't sure. The only thing she did know was, the dress didn't feel safe.

But no matter how confusing her feelings were, she wasn't about to admit any sort of doubts to Cade. Where she'd come from, vulnerability was a weakness. Besides, they were late for the fund-raiser already.

"Never mind," she told him firmly. "It's too late to change, anyway. Just do me a favor and try to keep your weapons concealed for the rest of the evening. I'd rather not look down later and discover myself wearing a miniskirt. I've had about all the surprises I can stand for one week."

"Same here, sweetness," he said, holding open the front door. "Same here."

Twenty minutes later he was escorting her into the

museum lobby and down the hall toward the Caribbean room, where the fund-raiser was in full swing. As soon as they'd made an entrance, Cade took one quick look around and wondered if they were in the right place. If this was what Nick perceived as a party, she was even more repressed than he'd imagined.

The room was filled to capacity, but if anyone was having a good time, Cade couldn't tell. Socialites didn't necessarily smile when they were enjoying themselves. They just milled around slowly, bobbing their heads up and down at each other like a well-trained pack of dash-board dogs.

Cade kept one arm wrapped around Nick's waist and used the other to lift a glass of champagne from a passing tray. "Here," he said, handing it to her. "One of us is going to need this."

She took a careful sip, then looked up at him with a quick smile of gratitude. Cade felt something register deep within his gut. Something powerful and protective and totally unfamiliar. It was a feeling he didn't like one bit.

Ignore it, man, he told himself. *Ignore it or you're out of here. No Picasso. No reward. Just simple self-preservation.*

But the feeling just got stronger when one of Nick's friends had the nerve to approach. He was one of those tweedy types she seemed to think so much of—conservatively dressed and stuffy. A guy whose necktie was so tight, it had probably choked the life out of him long ago.

"Martinique," the man said. "You look lovely to-night."

Lovely? Cade wanted to laugh. It was the understatement of the year. She looked hotter than a four-alarm jambalaya, and Bozo here knew it. The guy was trying to play it polite, but he was practically leering at Nick's exposed leg.

Cade wanted to put his fist through the man's face.

Instead he dropped his arm from Nick's waist, shook hands with Bozo, and went off to work the room. But his eyes kept straying back to Martinique. And the man with her, poor jerk. It was obvious he thought he had a chance.

And maybe he did.

She was dancing with him now, if you could call it that. The orchestra was playing some poor excuse for music, and Nick was cocking her head to hear something he'd said, tilting her beautiful face back to laugh. Cade felt his stomach muscles fisting hard, as though someone had just punched him in the solar plexus.

It took everything he had not to cut in on Mr. Clean and tell him to take a hike. But Nick didn't need him at the moment. She seemed to be enjoying herself. And Cade had to force himself to remember his reason for being there.

He headed for the back of the room, where a no-cash casino had been set up for the evening's festivities. The high rollers were there, playing for points and prizes. No money was changing hands, but Cade could still smell action all the same. And when dollars and drinks were flowing freely, information was sure to follow. He bought a fistful of chips and made his way toward the blackjack table.

Martinique felt her stomach sinking as the back of Cade's broad shoulders finally disappeared into the crowd. He'd deserted her. So much for being rescued by a knight in shining armor. Or a biker in black. Cade probably figured she could look after herself. And she could, of course. She'd come alone to these functions plenty of times. She hadn't even wanted to bring Cade along tonight. So why was she feeling so let down?

"Martinique," her dancing partner prompted, giving her shoulders a gentle shake, "is something wrong?"

She brought her eyes guiltily back to Dennis Harold's forehead and smiled. She couldn't quite bring herself to look him in the eye. She was afraid her disappointment would show too clearly, so she concentrated on his hairline instead, counting the neat little rows where Dr. Curtis, the town's most expensive plastic surgeon, had done his most meticulous transplant work.

Hairplug Harold, the museum members called him. Poor Denny. He'd looked just fine before the operation. Now he looked perfect. Too perfect. With every hair shaft exactly in place, like a living Ken doll, fresh from the factory.

"Maybe you'd like to sit this next one out," he suggested. "Why don't I go get us a couple of soft drinks?"

"Thanks," Martinique agreed. "I must be getting tired."

Or going insane very slowly. What was the matter with her, anyway? Dennis Harold was a very nice guy. A well-respected corporate attorney with a fine reputation. He was safe and stable. The kind of man who'd be a good provider. So what if he was follically challenged? So what if the sound of his voice made her want to sleep standing up? She was far from perfect herself.

She'd pulled herself together by the time Denny returned. A good thing, because he'd brought one of the most formidable board members back with him. Lizanne Smith, a forty-something social jet–setter with the oldest husband and the biggest bank account this side of the Mississippi.

"Ms. Duval," she said, taking Martinique by the shoulders and planting two perfunctory pecks on either side of her face, "It *is* good to see you again. And you do look *stunning* tonight. Not that *I* could pull off a dress like that at *my* age, but it does look smashing on you."

Martinique thanked her, but she didn't miss the irony of the woman's words. Lizanne didn't look the least bit old. And her décolletage was the most daring in the room. The brilliant blue neckline plunged so low across her breasts and shoulders, parts of her looked ready to pop out. Luckily for Lizanne, she could get away with it. This town would tolerate a lot from someone whose family went all the way back to plantation times.

Still, Martinique had always liked the lady. She had spirit and an intelligent sparkle behind her flashing hazel eyes. All the gossips had said she'd married the old man just to get her hands on his fortune. But something about Lizanne made Martinique believe he'd gotten his money's worth.

They were still exchanging small talk when Cade finally returned. Lizanne's eyebrows went up immediately. Especially when Cade wrapped one long, powerful arm possessively around Martinique's shoulder.

"Miss me, honey?" he drawled in his smoothest Cajun accent. His voice was silky and low, just loud enough for Denny and Lizanne to hear.

Martinique wondered what he was up to. "Honey," he'd called her. The name was innocent enough. But the tone was intimate, seductive, faintly French. And as much as she liked the sound of the word and the way he'd spoken it, she knew it wasn't for her benefit.

For some reason, he wanted the whole room to know they were together. The signal was blatantly territorial. If he'd hung a sign around her neck reading Hands Off, it might have been more subtle. But Cade wasn't exactly the subtle type. And it didn't take Denny long to pick up on the clue. He excused himself suddenly, murmuring something about a soft-drink refill, and headed for the bar without a backward glance.

Martinique secretly wished the man had shown a little more backbone. It wasn't exactly flattering to have your only serious suitor take off at the first sign of trouble. But Cade Jackson did seem to have that effect on other men.

Women, on the other hand, seemed to attach themselves to him like magnets. Lizanne's gaze was still focused on him as intently as if he were the last available fudge brownie at a society bake sale.

"Martinique," she said, still keeping her eyes on

Cade. "It's positively criminal to keep a secret like this all to yourself. I hope you're going to introduce us."

Martinique made the necessary introductions, but Lizanne wasn't going to let her stop there.

"Details," the older woman insisted sweetly. "I need details, darling. Like, where did you find him? And how long have you two been an item?"

Martinique wasn't sure what to say. Cade was on the trail of a criminal, after all. They both were. And she didn't want to divulge any information that would put them in any more danger.

But she didn't want to give Lizanne the mistaken impression that they were an item, either. It simply wasn't true. It couldn't be. But as soon as she opened her mouth to set the record straight, Cade stepped in again and took control.

"I was knocked out at the sight of her," he told Lizanne. "Didn't even see it coming. We've been together ever since."

"Really?" Lizanne's gaze swept back and forth between them with growing interest.

Martinique groaned inwardly. Instead of putting the woman's curiosity to rest, Cade had only managed to pique it further. With Lizanne's love of "conversation," the news would be all over town in a matter of hours.

"Well, not exactly—" she started to tell Lizanne. But Cade cut in before she had a chance to finish.

"Nick promised me a dance tonight, and I'd like to take her up on it before the band decides to call it quits. Excuse us?"

"Of course," Lizanne murmured politely.

Martinique could feel her eyes following them as Cade swept her onto the floor and into his arms. She glared up at him hotly. "Why did you tell her that?"

He shrugged and pulled her flat up against him, guiding her movements with one hand positioned firmly at the base of her back and the other holding hers in an iron clasp. "She asked."

Martinique felt herself moving in his arms, very slowly. The orchestra number wasn't exactly a lively one, but what they were doing didn't seem active enough to be called dancing. It was more like a long, languorous hug. It was far too sensual a thing to do in public. And she was far too angry to enjoy it.

"She asked? Well, of course she asked! But you didn't have to insinuate that we . . . well, you know what I mean."

"Yes, I do know. And I think Lizanne caught my drift pretty well."

Cade watched her face flush hot and rosy. He wondered whether it was from anger or from excitement, then decided that most likely it was a little of both.

She stared up at him, green eyes flashing. "You did it on purpose!"

He nodded. "Now you're with me."

She tried to wrench her hand out of his grasp, but Cade wouldn't let her. For her sake, and for his, he couldn't let her make a scene. But he was enjoying himself more than he cared to admit. He liked the sight of her all stirred up. He liked the fact that she was strong enough and gutsy enough to stand up to him.

"I am not *with* you," she told him in no uncertain terms.

Cade didn't respond immediately, he just let some of her anger bubble over and simmer out. After a moment or two he could feel her relaxing against him, just a little. She was so close, he could feel the slow, erotic opening and closing of her skirt as she swayed to the music. He cursed himself for creating that slit in her dress. It was torturing him with every step she took.

"Whatever you say, Nick."

"And I don't see why Lizanne should think we're an item."

"Take it easy for a minute and I'll tell you."

She took a deep breath, exhaling slowly, then gave him an expectant stare. "Well?"

"It's for your own good. Picasso needs to know you're not alone."

"Picasso, maybe. But do you have to tell the entire town that we're . . . together?"

"Whatever happens here is likely to get back to him."

She eyed him skeptically. "I don't see how. Sicko, sadistic art thieves don't exactly mix with this museum's guest list."

"Don't be naive, Nick. You may think these muckety-mucks are all nice and law-abiding and above-board, but there's plenty of dirt to go around, even at an upscale shindig like this. It took me only twenty minutes of schmoozing to get the name and location of the French Quarter's favorite art fence. That's not exactly the kind of information you'd expect these pillars of the community to have handy in their address books."

She let out a soft gasp. "Someone here told you that? Who?"

"It doesn't matter. What does matter is that your world and his are more closely connected than you realize. We need to let the people here know those two paintings of yours are too hot to handle. Spread the word. Make them harder to fence."

She shook her head slowly. "I'll admit there's enough money here to buy those canvases a dozen times over on the black market. But it's hard to imagine that any of these people would. I know a lot of them. At least, we're acquainted professionally. We're friends in the same business circle. And now you're saying that some of them might be shady?"

"If these people were really your friends, Nick, you wouldn't be afraid to be yourself in front of them."

"I'm not afraid!" she insisted. "You don't understand. I just don't see why they should speculate about us, why they have to believe we're . . . a couple."

"Lovers," he corrected. "You don't see why they should think we're *lovers*. Funny thing, Nick, you do have a real knack for avoiding that word."

FIVE

Martinique felt her stomach muscles clench at the mere mention of the word. *Lovers.* Something went weak inside her at the sound of it on Cade's lips.

She couldn't help conjuring up the images that the unwelcome word provoked. Intimate images of herself and Cade doing exactly what the sound suggested. Doing more than she'd ever dreamed of with any man.

She didn't know where the thoughts had come from. She only knew she shouldn't be having them. She looked away, trying to focus on the far wall of the room, on anything that would take her mind off such a disturbing subject.

"I don't know what you're talking about," she told him. But she did, Lord help her. She knew he was right. It was a word she wanted to avoid at all costs.

"Right. And the fact that you can't look me in the eye has nothing to do with it either."

Stung by the accusation or, more importantly, by

the perfect accuracy of it, she forced herself to meet his gaze. "Lovers, sexual partners, use any term you like. I just prefer not to put it so bluntly."

His eyebrows arched in sharp amusement, as though he understood every wishful, unwilling thought he'd conjured up inside her. As though he could strip her defenses away with a single, penetrating glance. "So crudely, you mean. Is that the problem, Nick? Am I just a little too rough around the edges for a lady like you?"

"Rough on the reputation is more like it," she said. "This may sound a little old-fashioned, but I do care about mine. I'm the first woman in my family who *doesn't* have one. I'd just like to keep it that way."

"So I come along and shatter the illusion?" he asked. "Sorry to let you down, sweetness, but you should be thanking me for that. Life's too short to spend in the middle of a mirage. Reality's a lot more interesting."

"Your reality maybe," she said. "Not mine. This is a different world than the one I grew up in. Way different. I'm just trying to fit in." She stopped, trying to swallow against the painful ache in her throat. "Never mind. I don't expect you to understand."

"I know you don't. And it makes me wonder, Nick, why your expectations about men are so low."

She let out a short, involuntary laugh. "Realistic, you mean."

"What I mean is, you've got a protective wall around yourself so thick, dynamite wouldn't dent it. How's a man supposed to get in?"

She lifted her chin a notch, a little hurt by the un-flattering description. "He's not. That's the idea."

He laughed and let her go just as the music stopped. "Careful. Some men might see that as a challenge."

"A man like you, I suppose?"

They were still standing on the dance floor, waiting for the next number to begin. He reached down with one hand and tipped her chin up until their eyes met. "No," Cade told her frankly. "I'll admit I like a good chase now and then, but I prefer my women willing. If that's what you want, Nick, you'll have to make the next move yourself."

"In your dreams, Jackson."

He smiled. "If I remember right, that's just how it happened the last time."

Martinique glanced up from the ledger on her desk, distracted by the sound of chimes. The bronze mantel clock in the store's window display was sounding again, reminding her that the afternoon was growing late. As if she needed reminding.

As if she'd had a single moment of peace since Cade had taken off to find the art fence. It had been hours now. Hours since he'd roared off on his bike, promising to return before dark. With news of Picasso's where-abouts, if possible. With some clue about her paintings, if the luck was with them.

But so far she hadn't heard a word. And she was starting to worry. Not about Picasso or the possible re-covery of her property. She was worried about *him*.

He was all alone out there, tracking down trouble.

What if something awful had happened to him? What if he was hurt again and needed help? What if he never came back?

Just the thought of never seeing him again, never dancing in his arms again the way she had last night, made her feel strangely nauseous.

Heaven help her, but she'd enjoyed every minute of it. She'd tried not to. She'd tried to maintain a safe, professional distance. But it was impossible to stay completely detached with 180 pounds of pure, protective masculinity pressed up against you. Cade Jackson wasn't the kind of man you could easily ignore.

Or forget, unfortunately. No matter how much she wanted to. Dear Lord, was she falling for him already?

Didn't the attraction between them prove that she was every bit as easy as Angelé had been? Every bit as wild and weak, every bit as vulnerable to a bad boy with a beautiful face?

Or was she crazy enough to believe that things could be different for her?

The sound of voices coming from the front of the store drew her quickly out of the daydream. A young couple who'd been window-shopping their way down Royal Street stopped just outside her door, apparently debating whether or not to come inside.

Martinique understood their hesitation. Some antique shops were notorious for intimidating their customers. It had always amazed her, but unnecessary snobbery seemed to abound in the business. She'd made it a point, since the day her doors had first been opened, to welcome each and every client who crossed her threshold as graciously as possible.

Today was no exception. Martinique looked up from her desk and gave the couple an encouraging smile through the large glass window. She was rewarded for her effort when they finally mustered up the courage to come inside.

They were somewhere in their twenties, most likely tourists, judging by their summer shorts and the light-weight camera hanging from the woman's left arm. And they were obviously in love.

"We're looking for wedding bands," the man told her. "We noticed a pair in your window. Are they antique?"

Martinique confirmed that they were over one hundred years old, probably mid-Victorian, based on the style and the jeweler's hallmark stamped inside. She took them out of the window so that the couple could try them on.

"They're beautiful," the woman murmured. "Delicate. Oh! Mine's engraved inside. *Forever yours.*"

Martinique explained that the Victorian culture had been a particularly sentimental one. Queen Victoria's adoration for her husband, Albert, had set a sweet, romantic tone for most of the nineteenth century.

But her customers weren't paying too much attention to her impromptu art history lesson. They were so involved in the rings, in the way they fit, and in each other, she felt it was intrusive to disturb them any further.

"Take your time," she suggested, and backed off a

little, giving them an opportunity to discuss the potential purchase. "It's a big decision."

It's *forever*, she thought. For always.

And it would never be for her.

Had she actually imagined, just a few minutes ago, that she and Cade might have some kind of future together? Had she forgotten so quickly that the Duval women were notoriously bad at picking potential mates?

Had she forgotten that men like Cade weren't the committing kind?

It was probably the party last night that had led to her temporary lapse in sanity. All that talk about the two of them being lovers. Luckily, though, she'd come to her senses in time.

"We'll take them."

Martinique felt herself smiling mechanically, slowly coming out of the fog. "Excuse me?"

"We'll take them," the man repeated. "The rings. And thanks for being so patient with us. For all your help."

Martinique wrote up the sale and sent the couple happily on their way, thanking them repeatedly for their patronage. She *was* especially grateful. Not only had they made a significant purchase from her, but they'd shown up at the store at a particuarly providential moment, forcefully reminding her of her own priorities.

Adora would say it was the spirits, the *orisas* and other strange, mysterious forces in action, that nothing in life was left to chance. But whatever it was, when Cade finally returned a few minutes later, Martinique knew she'd been saved in the nick of time.

If she hadn't so recently renewed her resolve to stay a safe distance, she might have been tempted to rush forward and fling her arms around him.

"Miss me, sweetness?"

God yes, she had. But she wasn't about to admit it. "Back so soon?" she asked, congratulating herself on how unconcerned she sounded.

He grinned and settled down into a French fauteuil, studying her. It was hard to read his exact expression behind the black stubble of five o'clock shadow and the dark gray aviator sunglasses, but Martinique had the distinct impression that she didn't fool him one bit.

He leaned back against the cushions and locked his arms behind his head, still watching her. "Aren't you going to ask me how my day was, honey?"

She flashed him an impertinent smile. "Maybe you'd like me to fetch you a beer first. Pull your boots off for you? Rub your neck?"

His white grin grew wider. "Sounds awesome, angel-face. When do we start?"

"When pigs fly. Where have you been?"

"Around." He looked pleased with himself. "You did miss me, didn't you?"

"Dream on. Did you find the fence?"

He lowered his sunglasses and looked at her over the rims. "More or less. I set up a meeting time for tonight. Eleven o'clock at one of the local clubs."

"Good," she said, pleased that he'd made some kind of progress. "I'm going with you."

He took the glasses off completely and shook his head. "Sorry, sweetness. It's not going to happen."

"You won't take me? Why not?"

He didn't respond immediately. "Let's just say it's not a very nice place."

"Is that all?" she asked, relieved. "Well, don't worry about me. I can handle not very nice. I won't blow it if you let me come along. I might even be able to help."

He shot her a long, speculative look, rubbing one hand slowly across the stubbled darkness of his chin. "I don't know, Nick. This isn't your run-of-the-mill dance club that sells visual sex. The entertainment is more on the kinky side. They do tattoos, body piercing, that kind of stuff."

"Oh," she said, a little shocked in spite of herself. "Well, how bad can it be? I've seen tattoo parlors before. Of course, I've never actually been in one, but—"

"This place isn't as private as a parlor. The crowds can get pretty big. And everyone likes to watch."

"To watch? Watch what?"

"The art in action. The subtle accentuation of the human form. And the not-so-subtle. Apparently, the body piercing is the most popular."

She made a disgusted face, throwing all pretense of worldliness to the wind. "You mean they all stand around gawking while people get pierced and tattooed?"

He nodded. "That pretty much sums it up."

Martinique shook her head in amazement. "Well, I just don't get it. It's perverse. Public mutilation. Why would anybody want to watch some unfortunate schmoe get stabbed with a needle?"

Cade shrugged. "Who knows? Society's search for a

new low? A raunchy rite of passage? All I know is, it's the fence's favorite hangout and he's going to be there at eleven. Spilling his guts to me."

"How can you be so sure? How do you know he'll trust you enough to talk about Picasso?"

"It's my business to know, babe. Besides, I already met the guy this afternoon. He's on the verge of making a major revelation, but he wants to be sure I'm not going to haul *him* back to jail when I bust his buddy. He wants proof that I'm a badass bounty hunter out to make a buck and not an undercover cop. And I'm going to give it to him."

"How?"

A swift hint of a smile crept into the corners of his eyes. "By doing something no cop in his right mind would do just to make a deal. I'm going to have a body part pierced. *I'm* going to be the unfortunate schmoe who gets stuck with the needle tonight."

Martinique blinked in disbelief. "You're joking."

He folded his arms across his chest, cool, determined, and dangerously stubborn. "I'm as serious as a mobile home owner in the middle of a hurricane."

"But—don't you think it's a little extreme?"

"Could be," he agreed, inclining his head with a short, single nod of assent. "But extreme is the only thing that will work with this crowd. A simple bribe and a gentleman's promise aren't enough to impress them."

"Are you sure it's worth it? I mean, it's going to hurt, isn't it? They're going to stick a needle in your . . . in your . . ."

Exactly what part *were* they going to stick a needle

in? His ear? His nose? His . . . ? She wasn't sure she wanted to know.

Luckily, Cade spared her the embarrassment of asking. "Navel," he said bluntly.

"Oh," she whispered. "In your navel. I see." And she did. Very graphically. It made her wince just thinking about it.

"Frankly, it sounded a lot less painful than the other options. You wouldn't believe all the parts they're piercing these days."

"Please." She shuddered. "I'd rather not hear about them. The navel is bad enough."

"It should be," he agreed.

"You can't do it," she stated flatly. "I won't let you."

He gave a low, indulgent laugh, as if she were a defiant child he didn't have the heart to discipline. "You won't let me?" he asked softly. "Sweetness, you can't stop me."

She flushed warmly, realizing just how ridiculous her own words had sounded. How personal. How possessive. Cade Jackson could go and have *Easy Rider* tattooed across his forehead for all she cared. He could get a gold ring in his nose and it wouldn't faze her one bit.

"I didn't mean it that way," she said, struggling for an explanation. "I know I don't have any kind of hold on you. I just meant—I hope you're not doing this for my sake—to protect me from Picasso. I wouldn't want you to go that far for me."

"Thanks for the concern, angel-face, but this isn't all for you. I *really* want to get this guy."

He was almost smiling when he spoke, but the expression in his eyes grew suddenly lethal, making Martinique draw in a quick breath. It was a cold look, almost chilling in its intensity. A look that promised to take no prisoners.

She noticed the muscle working in his jaw and realized that he was struggling with some very strong emotions. Pain? Anger? She wasn't sure.

But her heart went out to him. Her heart ached for him. And she suddenly understood why he was willing to be bashed over the head with whiskey bottles, or wake up in gutters, or get his perfectly good navel pierced in some sleazy exhibitionist bar. She suddenly understood that Cade's quest for criminals was more than a way to make a living or simply survive.

It was personal.

"So do you still want to come along?" he asked. "It should be quite a show."

Cade stood alone in the shadowy courtyard, jean-clad, barefoot, drink in hand, and watched the evening gaslights come on along Royal Street, one by one. It was his favorite time of day, the sultry, shadowed interval between light and darkness, when the afternoon was finished and the promise of the night still stretched before him, full of mystery. It made him think of a woman, dark haired, cloaked in velvet, unfolding her arms to take him in.

It made him think of Martinique. But then, so did everything these days.

The haunting waves of a jazz trombone rolled

toward him from some far corner of the French Quarter. *Le coeur de la cité*. If this was the heart of the city, then music had to be its pulse.

Whether it was slow and sensual, like the elusive strains of jazz, or blatantly ear blasting, like the decadent jungle drumbeat of a Caribbean band, this town swayed to its tunes with total abandon. It was a place of wild contrasts, where the culture was as saturated as the climate, ranging from cool, to sweltering, to anything in between.

Sin City. She was sophisticated by day, sexual by night. She offered everything a man could desire and more.

So much like *her*.

He gave a hard sigh, tipped his head back, and drained the contents of his drink. Dark rum seared a scorching path down his throat, making the moisture bead lightly along his temples. He hoped the fire of it would burn him up inside, turning the smoldering need within him to ashes. The need for Nick.

She was seducing him slowly, the same way this city had. Unconsciously. Without even trying. Giving him glimpses of her strength, her resilience, her raw, sweet wildness, but keeping them hidden behind a cool, cosmopolitan mask.

It was that inner sanctuary he wanted access to. But it was locked up, shut tight, as carefully closed off as the wrought-iron gate before him and the beauty of the courtyard it barred. Teasing him to explore. Making him want her.

And it had been a very long time since he'd wanted

anything at all other than the hunt at hand and whatever lay ahead. Maybe that was why he'd agreed to the meeting tonight, agreed to go through with this ridiculous ritual to prove himself to the fence. It was a little over the edge, he realized. Not that he hadn't gone down that road before. Not that he hadn't walked on the wild side too many times in the past. But this time he wanted to take the quickest route, to get the task accomplished and get out.

And if it took a little minor physical pain to move things along, it was worth it. If he could just get going again before he broke any more of his own survival rules. Before she got under his skin for good.

Before he found himself wanting to stay.

The Body Bazaar was everything Martinique had expected—dark, opulent, and eerie, with the walls draped entirely in black and only the sparkle of a breathtaking baroque chandelier to relieve the room's strange austerity. White candles were clustered at every table, their golden flames throwing shadows in the faces of the club's numerous, nameless patrons.

But the focal point of the room by far was the small black stage at the front. It was empty now, except for the single row of candles guttering along its length, presumably taking the place of footlights. Ominously empty.

Martinique didn't have to ask what the stage was for. She knew. A quick anticipatory shudder snaked its way down her spine.

A scantily clad hostess, wearing what appeared to be only the top half of a very tight, very red cancan costume, led her and Cade to their front-row table for two. Her sense of foreboding grew as she noticed that the other patrons were watching their entrance with interest and that many of them wore feathered or sequined Mardi Gras masks, in spite of the fact that carnival season was far behind them.

She took a deep breath to calm herself and caught the sweet, musky scent of incense, dark and clinging. Even the smell of the place was faintly sinister.

Cade made a brief signal to one of the waitresses, who was wearing even less than the cancan girl, and drinks were on the table only a minute later. The woman's black rubber bustier further endowed what was an already voluptuous body, and when she bent over to serve them, a large red rosebud tattooed across her right breast came fully into view. Clearly, the show was meant for Cade's eyes, but Martinique had a hard time not staring herself, and an equally hard time handling the let's-get-it-on look that Rosebud shot at Jackson.

It was positively carnal. Martinique had a sudden urge to take the tall drink she'd just been handed and give Rosebud a long, thorough watering. She'd bet that little rubber top was watertight enough to hold a pitcher or two of liquor and ice.

But much to her relief, Cade sent the woman on her way with no more than a faint smile and a generous tip. Either floral-embossed breasts weren't much to his liking, or he was so used to being flirted with that a little overt body language just wasn't enough to get a reaction.

"Drink okay?" he asked.

She took her first sip of the unfamiliar concoction. It was full of fruit nectar, vodka, and rum, laced with a hint of apricot brandy, covered with crushed ice and topped with a twist of lime. She nodded her approval. It was nice, but a little too potent for her taste. Obviously not for lightweights.

"A Devil's Tail," Cade told her.

She took another careful swallow, feeling a little light-headed already. "How appropriate. When does the sacrifice begin?"

A faint drumbeat started in the background, lending a strange, premonitory emphasis to her words. It was mixed with a primitive, tribal kind of music, sharp and percussive, with strings and chimes and other odd instruments Martinique couldn't begin to name. A high-pitched human element ran through it, half chant, half wail, that made the hair at the back of her neck begin to tingle.

Cade seemed to sense her anxiety. "You don't have to watch this," he told her. "You can still back out."

She swallowed hard. "I will if you will."

"Too late," he said, shaking his head. "A man's word. It's the code of the road."

Martinique sighed in exasperation. Now was not the most sane moment for Cade's nobility to surface. She wanted to drag him bodily from the room, to warn him about the terrors of torn flesh and the risk of gruesome skin infections, and all he could talk about was some crazy, unwritten law. Some macho rule for rough guys.

"I just don't get it," she told him. "How can you think of honor at a time like this?"

He shrugged, but his voice was smooth and reassuring. "Sit tight, Nick. It'll be over soon."

The rising crescendo of the music put an end to any further conversation between them. The anticipation of the crowd began to mount as all attention turned toward the empty stage. The curtains parted. A man stepped out. And suddenly the room was silent.

Martinique stared at the man in shock. Except for a small black thong slung low around his pelvis, he was naked. But it wasn't the sight of so much unclothed flesh that surprised her. It was the color of it. Or rather, the colors.

He was multihued from head to foot—completely covered with tattoos.

The bold, bright designs glowed against his skin like the dark, outlined patterns in a stained-glass picture window. Flowers and stars, eagles and flags, demons and dinosaurs all fought for space on the same living canvas of skin. It was beautiful and hideous all at once. He struck a pose for the audience, strutting to the sound of admiring applause.

Martinique took a long drink of her Devil's Tail. She'd thought she'd seen it all before. She'd been wrong.

She glanced over at Cade, wondering what his reaction would be to the strange spectacle, and realized with sudden horror that he was gone. She made a frantic visual search of the room, but there was no sign of him. He'd simply vanished.

One look up at the stage only increased her alarm. The tattooed man was gone and in his place stood a tall figure, black cloaked and heavily hooded.

"Doctor Demented!" someone shouted. "Give 'em hell, Doc!"

Doctor Demented? Martinique wondered. The man looked more like a cross between the grim reaper and a hideous, hungry vampire than any doctor she'd ever seen. He definitely wasn't wearing a white lab coat or a reassuring, sterile smile.

An assistant appeared on stage, rolling a small stainless-steel cart. When Doctor Demented held his hands out, the man helped him don a thin pair of latex surgical gloves. Martinique felt slightly better seeing that some effort was being made to keep the procedure sanitary. But when Doctor Demented selected a long silver needle from the assistant's tray, holding it high in the air for everyone's inspection, she felt her stomach suddenly queasy.

Was *that* what they used to pierce human flesh? It was nothing like the quick, neat piercing gun she remembered from having her ears done. That thing was a weapon, huge and horrifying, nearly three inches long from base to tip!

"Come on, Doc!" a man in the audience yelled impatiently. "Let's see some blood!"

A chorus of encouraging whistles and catcalls went around the room as the curtain parted. And Cade walked out on stage.

SIX

"It's *him*," Rosebud breathed near Martinique's shoulder. "The one they call Cowboy. The wild one. This I have to see."

Martinique couldn't spare a glance at the woman. She was too busy watching the stage, transfixed, as Cade pulled his shirt off in one smooth, easy stretch. She heard herself gasp, along with the rest of the audience, and felt a sharp thrill course through her at the sight.

Lean, magnificent muscles flexed and corded beneath his deeply tanned skin, dormant but deadly. A dark vee of chest hair curled closely across his pecs and sternum, dropping to a sharp, sensual point as it snaked below his hips and disappeared suddenly into the low-slung belt of his blue jeans. He hooked two fingers in his belt loops and strode casually toward the figure in black.

Somewhere below the anxious ache in her throat, Martinique felt her admiration rise. Cade didn't look like a man who was summoning up his courage. He didn't look brave. He looked fearless.

The crowd ate it up. A cheer sounded, along with several hisses and catcalls. "Use the handcuffs, Doc!" someone yelled. "He's got muscle! He might put up a fight!"

Cade's arms were drawn behind his back and securely shackled. Rosebud let out an excited whisper. "He *is* a strong one."

Martinique's heart went a little crazy at that point. There was something horrifying and fascinating about the scene, all at the same time. Something mesmerizing about Cade, handcuffed, half naked, and completely at the mercy of the demon Doc. Something strong and seductive in the power of his stance.

Anticipation stretched inside her, wire taut.

Doctor Demented lifted his arms in the air, conjuring slowly. From the dark folds of his left sleeve, he produced a bottle of something clear and strong. Vodka? Gin? Martinique couldn't quite make it out in the murky blackness of the bar.

Dramatically, playing to the audience, Doctor Demented raised the bottle to Cade's lips and offered him a drink.

"Go ahead, man!" someone in the audience shouted. "You're gonna need it!"

Cade declined and told the Doc to get on with it.

The crowd went wild.

Martinique felt a little faint. She wished he'd taken the alcohol, just for the anesthetic effect. She wished *she'd* taken it. She wished he didn't look quite so sexy standing there, more amused than afraid. He was so brave, so ruggedly beautiful, she wanted to melt.

Doctor Demented took a hemostat from the cart and prepared to operate, clamping Cade's flesh with the long, skin-tightening tongs. He raised the needle in the air again, leveling it dead center at Cade's gut, at the sinewy, shadowed spot that marked the middle of his stomach plane.

The crowd went crazy. "Do it," they chanted. "Do it, do it!"

Martinique's heart was in her throat by now, the anticipation so strong, she could barely swallow. It was total, trembling agony, but as excruciating as it was to watch, it was just as impossible to turn away. Her neck muscles were tight with tension, her temples damp, but she couldn't take her eyes off Cade.

He was scanning the audience, a suggestion of a smile in his bayou blue eyes, searching for something, for someone. For her. Their eyes locked and held. *No sweat, sweetness*, his expression said. *Here's the easy part.*

And in another instant it was over. There was a sharp stab from the needle, a quick grin from Cade, and the crowd was on its feet, cheering.

Martinique watched the spectacle in amazement. The Doc was inserting a small golden ring in the wound as the Bazaar's patrons moved toward the stage en masse, chanting at Cade in raucous approval. The conquering warrior, Martinique mused. A navel hero.

She was so relieved it was over, so exhausted from the anticipation, she didn't feel much like staying for the festivities. And Cade didn't look as though he'd be finished anytime soon. It would take hours for him to ward off all the women, she realized, not to mention the fact that he still had to speak to the fence. She made a quick decision, slipped quietly out of the club, and caught a cab for home.

Five minutes later the driver dropped her off at her courtyard entrance. Yawning, she waved him off and turned to unlatch the gate.

She heard the voice just as she stepped inside.

It was cold, sarcastic, and strangely familiar. "Welcome home, baby," he said. "Did ya have a nice night out?"

Martinique swore softly. She didn't have to see the face to remember the fear. It was a voice she'd never forget. Picasso.

He'd come back. And Cade was nowhere near.

"What's the matter?" he asked, taunting her. "No boyfriend here to protect you tonight?"

She looked down at her hands, at the keys she was still clutching, and realized that she was shaking. Shaking so hard the metal was rattling faintly between her fingers.

She drew in a quick breath, fighting for oxygen and the chance to keep her head clear. She'd done it once before, on the day he'd robbed her store. She'd stayed calm enough to survive. But it hadn't been so dark. And they hadn't been alone.

Tonight she was paralyzed. Riveted with primal fear, pure and simple. She wanted to scream, but no sound would come. She finally turned to run, but she didn't stand a chance. He slammed the gate shut in front of her.

"Not so fast," he hissed, his face still shaded, a menacing gray silhouette against the black wrought-iron bars. "I let you off easy last time. Didn't lay a finger on you, did I?"

Martinique realized he wasn't masked this time. He'd grown either more careless or more reckless since their last encounter. Both were hazardous, maybe even lethal. And it was frighteningly clear now, by his lack of precaution, that he *knew* she could identify him.

"Yeah," she said, her voice low and breathless, full of loathing. "You're a real nice guy."

"But you couldn't leave well enough alone," he added, stealing toward her in the shadows. "You and that crazy cowboy. He's on my case like a flea on a dog. Always itchin' at my back. Guess I need to mess you up a little, show him I can give trouble as good as I get. Show him how to keep his lady in line."

She gave him a scornful glance, hiding the rising terror inside. "You're not man enough."

He caught a handful of her hair and jerked her hard up against the iron gate. He was close behind her. So close, she could smell the stench of stale beer on his breath, feel the damp, sickening warmth of his body, sticky with sweat.

"Not man enough for you am I, baby?" he demanded. "And I suppose your big, bad boyfriend is?"

"Drop dead," she told him, and spat on the ground the way she'd seen Adora do it a hundred times.

"*Cochon*," she added, insulting him in French. "Filthy pig."

"Spirit," he said, slurring the word a little. "I like that in a woman. I like to cut it out of her."

The prick of something razor sharp teased across her throat, stroking at her skin, underscoring Picasso's ominous words. He was pressing a knife against her neck, drawing the point slowly from one ear to the other, almost scratching the tender surface. She felt his hand shaking with anticipation, felt the steel tip of the blade shivering in response.

A knife, Martinique knew, was Picasso's weapon of choice. And tonight he seemed all too eager to use it. Judging by the acceleration of his breathing and the excited trembling in his body, he was only seconds away from slicing her.

It was time to fight for all she was worth, to struggle to save her own life. Remembering the keys she still held in her hand, she wielded them tightly, raising them high over her head and down again, scraping hard against his face.

He howled in pain, enraged, loosening his hold on the knife, bringing his arm and elbow up to ward off the blows. Martinique took the opportunity to try to break free, twisting and writhing against him with all of her might. But it wasn't enough.

She was too weak. His grip on her was too hard. Luckily, the force that finally knocked him off balance was far stronger.

It was the force of the gate being flung open at warp speed by a big man in a very bad mood. The force of

Cade in a cold rage. It sent Picasso flying out onto the sidewalk, but it rocked Martinique back on her heels as well. She caught hold of a crevice in the courtyard wall and fought to remain upright.

The sight of Picasso squirming on the pavement left Cade with a single, overwhelming emotion—the need to kill. The urge to squash the stinking bastard like a wormy, writhing bug beneath his boot.

But it was the sheer strength of that need that stopped him. He might actually go through with it this time, he realized, and murder the man where he lay, with pleasure. Without the least bit of remorse.

He could almost feel Picasso's fragile neckbones breaking beneath his bare hands. But it wasn't justice he wanted this time. It was revenge. And he wanted it because of her.

She'd gotten away from him at the club, taking off so fast he'd barely had a chance to catch his breath and come after her. She'd scared the hell out of him, leaving like that. Didn't she realize what kind of trouble she could get herself into, a sweet thing like her all alone at night in a city like this?

But he'd had no idea of the danger she was in. Not until he'd reached the sidewalk outside her shop and heard her giving her attacker hell. He'd sensed the fear in her voice, and his heart had almost slammed to a stop.

Picasso, he decided, could wait until some other time. Martinique's safety was foremost on his mind right now. He turned to see if she was okay, and heard the perp's footsteps racing away behind him. The sound trailed off down the street, growing gradually fainter until it finally disappeared.

Cade didn't bother to look back. He picked the keys up from the ground where Nick had dropped them, shut the iron gate, and locked it tight. And then he went to her side.

She was leaning against the brick wall, shivering, her eyes still wide and wary with shock. "He's gone, *chérie*," he said, pulling her against him. "It's over for now. I'll take care of him later."

I'll kill him, Cade thought. *Just for laying his hand on you.*

She leaned into him heavily, shuddering, and Cade waited patiently until she stopped. She made him think of a small, fierce animal he'd wound up looking after by some twisted, miraculous mistake. Tough and tenacious when she was cornered, but soft and warm-blooded when he soothed her in his arms.

"Easy, angel-face." He led her over to the garden bench and settled down beside her. She rested against him again, content to let him calm her. "You're safe," he said, stroking her.

Which was more than he could say for Picasso. Or himself, for that matter. He was in trouble, he knew.

Up to his eyeballs. Over his head. Hell, he was in it so deep, he was standing at the bottom of the swamp.

And she had sent him there. For her sake, for his own, for the first time in his career, he'd actually let a perp go. *On purpose.* Practically handed him his walking papers.

Instead of stomping Picasso flat, he'd turned to

her—and broken every rule in the book. He'd had to know, right then, that she was all right, to convince himself the creep hadn't hurt her too bad. Because if she wasn't okay, he didn't think he could handle it.

The decision had been split-second, the kind he'd been used to making his entire career. Only this time he'd made the wrong one. This time he'd led with his gut instead of his head.

He'd finally lost his edge. Not because of a perp. Not because Picasso had beat him at his own game. He'd caved because of a woman.

"Nick," he said harshly, holding her tight. "Don't ever do that again. Don't leave my sight, *chérie*, until I can put him away permanently."

She nodded and made a muffled agreement, her face still buried in his chest. "Thanks," she sniffed, "for saving me."

"No problem," he lied. "Guess I owed you one. I'm just damn grateful I made it back here in time. Luckily, the fence liked the show so much, he didn't take long to talk."

She tipped her head back, glancing up at him wide-eyed, irresistibly curious. "What—what did you find out?"

"Enough," he told her. "Picasso's plenty pissed. Our trip to the museum was put to good use. The gossip's already gotten back to him."

"He must've heard about it," she agreed. "He called you my boyfriend."

Cade nodded. "The word is out about us *and* the artwork. Seems the paintings are going to be a hard sell for him now that most of the potential buyers know they're stolen. And know that everyone else knows it too. Our perp is holding merchandise that's nearly worthless, and he's not too pleased about it."

"Not too pleased?" she repeated, shivering. "Cade, I saw the look on his face. He's a maniac. I think he'd like to kill us. *After* he makes us suffer."

"Probably," he said. "But at least I can ID him now too. There's no reason for you to stay at risk. I can squirrel you away safely and take care of him alone."

"*Squirrel* me?" she asked, indignant. "Thanks a lot. And I suppose you think you might've handled everything alone up to this point?"

"Don't get riled, Nick. I didn't mean it that way. But a man's gotta do some things on his own."

"Like get himself killed?"

Cade frowned at that one, trying to figure out just what she was getting at. She seemed angry, somehow, but still concerned. Concerned for him? He couldn't remember the last time anyone had bothered over his welfare. The idea of Nick doing it now nearly blew him away.

"Or injured?" she added, drawing back as if she'd just remembered something. Hesitating, her hand clutched at the hem of his shirt. "I hope you didn't get hurt . . . down there."

"Down there?" he prompted.

"Your navel, remember? The site of your recent . . . operation. Throwing Picasso around like that might've made it bleed or something."

"Nope, it's fine." He pulled the bottom of his shirt up. "See for yourself."

The minute he glanced down and saw where her hands were headed, he realized his mistake. She was shy at first, tentative, like a hummingbird darting toward a flower, advancing, featherlight, then retreating. But the next thing he knew, she was touching him tenderly, running her trembling fingers along the edge of his jeans, fluttering over the small gold ring and the sore spot in the center of his belly.

"Is it uncomfortable?" she asked.

"Very."

"Sorry. Does it hurt when I touch you?"

"It's agony."

It was pure hell, having her hands on him like that. Every butterfly touch sent shafts of energy to his groin, tautening muscles, turning the heat up so high, she made his insides burn.

Her hair was massed against his throat and chin, enveloping him with its softness, surrounding him with a cloud of dark perfume, as black and bewitching as ritual incense. God, what had she done to him?

Conspired with that voodoo woman of hers, most likely, and turned him into a walking zombie. Black magic, that's what it was. Female magic. It swept everything inside him away, except the overpowering need of her.

The need to have her.

The need to recover what she'd taken from him so easily—his sanity and his will. He wasn't going to give them up without a fight.

She tipped her head back to look at him, and their gazes collided with a force that was almost physical.

"Sorry again," she whispered. "I just wanted to make sure you were okay. After rushing to my rescue like that . . ." Her voice trailed away.

She *should* be sorry. She was killing him. "Forget it. We're even now."

Even? Cade wondered. Who was he kidding? No matter who was keeping score, she was beating him, badly. She'd knocked the wind right out of him at the starting line. And she was still winning, even now, fanning the slow burn she'd started inside him, just by looking at him that way.

Like he was some kind of hero. Like his motives were pure and admirable instead of primitive and selfish. And very, very sexual.

"Almost even, angel-face." He wanted something more from her than a simple thank-you. More than misplaced hero worship. He wanted her unconditional surrender. To make her wild and wet with need. As hard up for him as she'd made him hard for her.

He caught hold of her wrist and held it. *He* would do the touching from here on out. She would be the one to feel it. The blinding ache, the white-hot heat, the exquisite agony, all of it.

He pressed her to the bench until she was flat on her back, until he was half on top of her. He brought his mouth within an inch of hers, forcing a soft moan out of her. But he didn't kiss her. He wouldn't kiss her this time. He wanted to hear her ask for it first. He wanted to hear her plead for their mutual pleasure.

He heard his own voice instead. He said her name, involuntarily, and she murmured his in response. Just the sound of it set him on fire. Muscles tightened, fisting far below his gut. He was rock hard already, and he'd barely even touched her.

Yet.

He slipped a hand beneath her dress, searching for the softness inside. The lace edge of her panties teased at his fingertips, scratchy and sensual. She whimpered, a sound so sexy it made his groin ache.

"Talk to me, *chérie*," he said. "Tell me how it makes you feel when I touch you."

"Crazy," she whispered. "Scared. Incredible."

His hand found her hot spot, and she arched beneath him. He stroked her there, slowly, rhythmically, milking the passion out of her until she went silky and slick with wanting. Until she gave a soft cry.

The proof of her pleasure inflamed him.

"You like it, sweetness," he said, his voice rough against her lips. "Don't you like it, *chérie*? Let me hear how much."

"Too much." Her voice broke from her throat in a ragged whisper. "I like it too much," she added on a sob. "Please," she begged him, clutching hard at his shoulders. "Please don't make me feel this way."

Cade couldn't make himself stop immediately. In fact, he didn't want to stop at all. But the pleas he'd finally wrenched from Martinique weren't the ones he'd originally had in mind. He'd wanted to make her hot, not unhappy. He'd wanted to make her wild, aware of her own passion, of the pleasure it could bring. Somehow he'd only managed to hurt her.

With an effort he tore himself away, forcing his body back to a sitting position on the bench. He raked a hand through his hair, struggling with the frustration and anger. Anger at her for the throbbing pressure in his groin, for the sweet, sharp need she'd conjured up inside him. Anger at himself for getting distracted again and losing control of this case so completely. For losing control of himself.

"It's pleasure, Nick," he said roughly. "Not pain. It feels *good*. It's jazz and jambalaya, cold beer and steamy summer nights all rolled into one. You're supposed to like it."

"Not like that," she told him quietly. "Not with you. This isn't supposed to be happening between us."

"So *I'm* the problem?" he asked, his voice harsh, angrier than he'd intended. "Sorry, sweetness, but I've never had any complaints before. Maybe your taste is just too refined. Maybe you like it better when that Denny geek tells you you're lovely and keeps a very safe distance while he's doing it. Well, you're not lovely, Nick. You're sin walking. Serious trouble on two legs. So don't expect me to keep a safe distance."

"You don't understand," she said. "I'm not like that. Not like the woman you just described. I *can't* be like her."

"At least not around a man like me," he added. "Tell me, Nick, what kind of guy really does it for you? Just who can you let go with, be yourself with? Dennis Harold, the lady's man? Mr. Perfect Catch himself?"

"There's nothing wrong with wanting a man like Denny," she insisted.

"Nothing at all," he agreed. "As long as you *do* want him. As long as the thought of neat and tidy sex really turns you on. Then Denny's your boy. You don't have to do a thing, don't have to *feel* a thing. I'll bet he can do it quick and clean, in five minutes flat. Without even messing your hair up. Am I right?"

"I wouldn't know. I never—" She stopped there, caught off guard in her anger, making him speculate about how the sentence might've ended.

I never *did it with Denny?* I never *did it with anyone?* He dismissed the latter as not being within the realm of reality. Nick was just too passionate, too much temptation to the male population at large to make him believe she'd never experienced sex before. Besides, she was so sensually responsive. She liked getting physical, he was sure. She just didn't like it with him.

But as tough as that concept was to handle, it was a relief to know that Dennis Harold hadn't had her. For some reason, just the thought of that had made him physically sick.

Careful, man, he warned himself. *Jealousy's not one of the survival rules.*

Most of his anger had burned itself out by now. Concern for Nick's welfare had taken its place. Concern mixed with guilt for putting her at risk with the perp. It was partly his fault she'd been in danger. He should never have let her out of his sight with Picasso still at large. He wouldn't let it happen again.

"Forget it," he told her. "We can settle that score later. Right now I need to get you away from here."

"Away? Still trying to squirrel me? Is that what you mean?"

He tucked his hand firmly under her chin and held her gaze. "I mean I'm taking you outta here, tonight. To someplace safe."

"Some . . . That's crazy. I can't leave. I have responsibilities."

"Don't we all, sweetness. That's why I'm telling you to pack your bags. Pronto."

She broke eye contact with him, shaking her head. "Get real, Jackson. I can't just up and go away with you."

Her tone held a trace of cool incredulity, and her chin went up, indignant. She was no-nonsense Nick again. Stubborn, independent, and hard to control.

Just the way he liked her.

He didn't resist the urge to egg her on. "Can't or won't?"

"What's the difference? We're not leaving."

"Afraid of what might happen?"

"Of course not." Her green eyes flickered with hesitation. "I mean, yes. What about my shop? What about Ming and Ching? Who's going to take care of them?"

He shrugged. "If that's all that's stopping you, leave a note. I'm sure your assistant can handle the shop for a few days. And that witch woman's always hanging around the apartment, anyway. Can't she feed the cats?"

"Well, yes," Martinique assented. "But don't call

Adora that! She's my housekeeper and also one of the best friends I've ever had."

"Fine," he agreed. "So all that's settled. Your help can hold down the fort. Unless you're worried about something else. . . ."

"I'm *not* worried."

"Good. Then let's go."

"Right now?"

"Now, Nick. Go grab some clothes, whatever you can fit in one *small* bag. The bike leaves in five minutes."

"For where?"

The suspicious tone in her voice told Cade she had some idea what was coming. But she didn't know the half of it. He broke it to her bluntly. "My place."

The look of shock that registered on her face made him smile. Score one for surprise, sweetness.

SEVEN

Cade's motorcycle raced westbound on Interstate 10, streaking through Baton Rouge, past the Atchafalaya Basin, and finally banking south into the steaming heart of Cajun country. Martinique swayed into the sharp turn, her arms drawn tightly around Cade's waist, her legs locked hard behind his as she stared out at the swampy scenery and hung on for all she was worth.

Thick canopies of gnarled cypress and live oaks passed overhead, silhouetted with silver moonlight, draped in Spanish moss, like ancient, ghostly Christmas trees dripping gray icicles of angel's hair. Startled by the approaching engine, snow-white egrets took suddenly to wing, rising silently from the treetops, pale and fluid as feathered spirit guides soaring toward the stars. A low-lying fog misted the ground for miles, hiding the hard surface beneath them, adding to the illusion that they were flying too.

Straight into an eerie, murky world Martinique

knew nothing about. Into a wild, brackish bayou with a man she understood even less. Cade Jackson.

He was riding them into the night on pure will and horsepower, like a Cajun cowboy on a dark, speeding stallion, gunning for home. Hell-bent for the dead center of nowhere. With her behind him.

What was she doing? He was the one who belonged here. He maneuvered the meandering curves and mossy byways as surely and stealthily as the Choctaw, Chickasaw, and Chitimacha Indians who'd come here before him. His fists gripped the handlebars with taut, tensionless control, his eyes guiding them onward with the sharp acuity of the all-seeing eagles that screamed overhead.

Martinique was merely praying they'd reach their destination in one piece.

"Almost there," he called back to her, as though reading her thoughts.

Or maybe it was the airtight, Tupperware squeeze she had on his waist that clued him in. She'd been plastered against him like paste on wallpaper ever since they'd left the main road. Riding on the highway had been a breeze compared to this curvy, mud-covered, marshland path.

The bike banked again, tipping far to the left, and Martinique's hands slipped down around Cade's hips. She caught hold of hard male angles, of raw, sleek muscle stretched across narrow pelvic bones. She jerked away involuntarily, almost losing her balance.

"Hang on!" he yelled over his shoulder.

Wasn't that what she'd been trying to do? There just

didn't seem to be any safe part of him to hang on to. Every touch between them seemed charged now, every accidental contact reminding her of the unspeakable intimacy they'd shared only hours ago. Just the memory of it brought a warm flush to her face that had nothing to do with the wind whipping softly at her skin.

Never, ever, had a man explored her so boldly, so suddenly, without any warning whatsoever. Without so much as a kiss to begin with, or any other polite pretense of foreplay. He hadn't asked or coaxed or cajoled her into submission. He'd simply taken it as his right, catching her completely off guard.

He'd set her on fire in seconds.

He'd reached into the very center of her being and stroked her straight to her soul. And she had loved it, every sweet, terrible, exciting thing he'd done. She'd loved it so much, it scared her.

Didn't that prove that she was a Duval woman down to the core? Another hopeless case of hormones around cocky heartbreakers like Cade? What had he called her? *Sin walking.* Was it that easy to read on her face the fact that she'd wanted to stray with him?

God, how she'd wanted it.

How she'd wanted *him*.

"You can pry your fingers loose now, Nick. We made it. Alive."

She blinked into the darkness, suddenly realizing that they'd come to a complete stop. "Oh! We're here? In one piece?"

He swung his leg over the bike and cocked the kickstand, a wry smile tilting at the edges of his mouth. "In two pieces," he confirmed. "Must be a miracle."

She let out a shaky sigh of relief, slid cautiously off the seat, and looked around. And saw nothing but swamp. Nothing but trees enveloped in misty tendrils, a small patch of sand beneath her feet, and moonlight melting into marshy wetland water. It was breathtakingly beautiful, like a French impressionist painting in a hundred spooky, sensual shades of silver and gray.

But hauntingly lovely as it was, it was still a bog. And they were still practically stranded in this dark, deserted countryside. And she wasn't sure she liked the idea one bit. Not at this time of night. Not just the two of them.

"A house," she said, "that's a miracle. You know, four walls, some electricity, a place to sleep. Only, I don't see a house. Did you take a wrong turn back there or something?"

He unstrapped her floral canvas duffel bag from the back of the bike and proceeded to make off into the trees with it. "No mistake," he promised her. "We take an alternative form of transportation from this point."

She followed him down the long, overgrown path, tracking close behind until a clearing broke at the edge of the undergrowth. She stared out at the smooth, unbroken stretch of black water. "Something tells me it's not going to be a nice, plush paddlewheeler."

He pointed to a ridiculously small canoe, propped upside down against a patch of woody cypress knees. "Unless you'd prefer to swim, which I don't advise at night. Too many gators."

Martinique did not prefer to swim. She helped him

flip the canoe over, and soon they were gliding toward the opposite side of the water. Toward his place, presumably. She glanced warily down at the water, searching for any sign of glowing alligator eyes, then back up at the horizon, trying to make out their ultimate destination. "At least there *is* a house," she murmured. "There is, isn't there?"

"See for yourself," he said behind her, slowing the narrow craft to a crawl. "It ain't much, but it's all mine. Home, sweet home."

And then she saw it, pale, puny, and pitiful in the moonlight. A small, rickety structure, gray and nondescript, perched ten feet above the waterline on narrow, spindly stilts. It was tinier than she'd imagined, no more than a one-room, tin-roofed crackerbox of a cottage. What there was of it seemed to be tacked together with rough, weathered boards and suspended precariously in midair, like a shaky, stork-legged treehouse sans tree.

"Now I know why you brought me here," she told him. "It's so secluded, no crooks can find the place. And the house is up so high, no one can get in there without wings. Including us."

"Sure we can," he assured her. "No sweat. See that rope ladder hanging along the left side?"

She saw it all right, by the light of the moon. It was dangling loose over the edge of the structure, a symmetrical series of sailor's knots rigged roughly between a double strand of rope. The heavy cord was frayed in spots, brittle, sun bleached, and of doubtful age.

She swallowed hard. "You're kidding, right?"

Apparently he wasn't. He headed the canoe straight

for the ladder and, with a few swift docking maneuvers, drew up alongside it. "Climb up," he said. "I'm right behind you. As soon as I secure the boat."

"Isn't there some other way in?" she asked hopefully. "Like an elevator? Some stairs, even?"

"Nope. That's the beauty of it. It's simple, no-frills security. Once the rope's up, you're safe. Don't even have to lock the front door."

"Assuming I make it to the front door."

"You'll make it," he said, reassuringly. "If I have to carry you."

"You wish," she shot back, and latched on to the ladder, determined to make the precarious ascent at all costs.

Miraculously, she reached the top without any of her anticipated disasters occurring. The rope didn't break. She didn't plunge, feet first, into black, gator-infested water. The ladder barely even swayed under her.

She pulled herself onto the narrow porch and stood, smoothing the tiny scraps of fiber from her hands. Cade followed moments later. He dropped her bag on the porch, drew the ladder up, and struck a match on the heel of his boot, lighting an old kerosene lamp that had been stashed by the door.

The flame flickered and leaped as he adjusted it, illuminating his eyes until they glowed a mysterious sapphire blue. Giant shadows loomed against the little house, dancing darkly, all the way up to the roofline.

Martinique shivered, chilled by the damp and the mist. "Guess this means there's no electricity."

Cade flashed her a quick grin. "Lucky guess. But we do have running water. And a very convenient outhouse around the other side. I spared no expense."

"A regular palace," she responded dryly.

He unlatched the door and led her inside. "It all depends on how you look at it."

When Martinique stepped over the threshold into the single, simple room, cozy was the first word that came to mind. Followed shortly by "togetherness." And "isolation."

It wasn't the size of the space that worried her, or the informal, purely functional decor, rather it was the overwhelming intimacy of the situation. The idea that she and Cade would be playing house here, all alone in the middle of a wild, steaming swamp. The fact that they would be sharing everything.

The carved wooden table flanked by two spartan chairs. The tiny corner of a kitchen with its crude, can-filled cupboard and wood-burning stove. The single picture, a human target poster riddled with bullet holes, all of them fatal, tacked on the wall with the point of a bowie knife.

The bed.

In Martinique's mind it dominated everything else in the room. Mainly because it was the only one in the room. One of it, two of them. She wasn't sure she liked the odds.

"I think I'll be going now," she told him, turning back toward the door.

"Hold on." He grabbed her by the back of the collar

and spun her around to face him. "You'll be needing these." He dropped a set of keys in her hand. "For the bike. Or my truck, if you can get it to start. It's parked just over there, beyond the big stand of oak trees. Good luck, Nick. I'm going to bed."

He released her and strode toward the other side of the room, seating himself on the edge of the mattress. He started to strip off his boots, one at a time. The shirt came next. He stood and eased it over his head in a single, unceremonious movement. The jeans were last. He unsnapped them and Martinique waited, swallowing back a helpless sound as they dropped to the floor in a pile.

He sank back on the bed, still in jockey shorts, and made himself comfortable beneath the covers. When she didn't make a move to leave, he spared a glance in her direction. He pulled the blanket back and invited her to join him with a clear, unmistakable crook of his finger.

Martinique still didn't move.

"Well? What's it gonna be, angel-face? My way or the highway?"

She glanced longingly at the bed, at the warm blanket, the inviting sheets, so unexpectedly clean and white. She *was* tired. She was so exhausted, she couldn't think straight. But she wasn't going to get under the covers with him even if mad swamp creatures tried to carry her off into the darkness.

She dropped the keys on the wooden table and settled into one of the wooden chairs, drawing her knees up against her chest. "Neither," she said. "You sleep. I'll stay up and keep watch."

"Suit yourself," he said, shrugging. "Don't forget the light." He stretched out on the bed again, yawning hugely.

Martinique blew the lamp flame out with a deep sense of regret and hugged her arms around her legs in a futile attempt to get warm. In an attempt to protect herself from . . . from what? From Cade? From what might happen if she let herself snuggle next to him, between the sheets?

Yes, from that. Definitely from that.

She heard his breathing grow regular and steady in the darkness. The sound of it brought her some sense of relief. She'd been granted a respite—for tonight, anyway. She rested her head against her knees and tried to get some sleep. The soft, chanting chorus of insects and frogs outside lulled her slowly into the darkness, into oblivion.

She woke with a start and a shiver. Her eyes flashed open as the wild beating of wings rushed overhead, accompanied by the blood-chilling call of a hawk. It was gone in moments, but she was wide awake by then, scanning the windows, the blackness outside, and imagining strange creatures lurking behind every one of them.

She wasn't sure how long she'd been asleep, but it was colder now. Much colder. She was freezing, and Cade was still snoozing, peaceful as you please, laid out as cool and completely relaxed as one of the legendary voodoo undead.

She wanted to shake him awake and beg him to light that lovely little wood-burning stove. She even considered lighting it herself, but visions of the shack in flames and the gators waiting for them below soon put that idea to rest. She settled for scooting her chair a little closer to the bed.

He wasn't shivering one bit. Maybe there was a draft in her part of the room. Maybe, if she was very deft about it, very quick and gentle, she could steal the blanket off him, just for a while.

A hoot sounded outside, followed by another horrible, hair-raising screech. She glared at Cade, amazed that rest could come so easily to him under such stressful, torturous circumstances. Didn't he understand that they were about to be attacked by flapping beast-monsters and huge, hairy-winged gargoyles?

Apparently not. Because his voice was very calm and clear when he finally called out to her.

"Come to bed, babe."

She heard the covers rustling as he pulled them back to make a spot for her beside him. Warmth. Just the idea of it almost had her sobbing with relief.

"To sleep," she insisted. "Nothing else. And at least one of us has to stay fully dressed at all times."

"Get in here," he demanded. "Now. One more argument and I feed you to the gators."

Martinique didn't open her mouth. Carefully, very carefully, she crawled in next to him. And sighed. And slept.

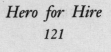

Cade woke early, the way he always did at home. If you could call a walk-in-closet–sized house that stayed empty for most of the year a home. Everything he had to show for himself was here, crammed into four hundred and fifty or so ramshackle square feet.

Not much.

But this morning it felt like paradise. Probably something to do with the woman nestled in his arms, soft, sleepy, and stuck to him tighter than peanut butter on jelly. She felt unbelievably right, lying in bed beside him. God, but she felt good.

So good, it was getting hard to remember why he'd brought her here. So good that *everything* was getting hard.

Keeping Picasso away, that was a piece of cake compared to the sweet torture of having Nick in the bed beside him. And *not* having her at all. He couldn't remember the last time this had happened to him—waking up with a woman after a night of uninhibited, abandoned . . . sleep. Hell, he wasn't sure it had ever happened.

She was definitely the first one he'd brought to this place. Nice motels were more his speed when he wanted to be alone with a woman. But the thought of taking Nick someplace like that just didn't sit right. She was too nice a lady for a nice motel.

He'd wanted to bring her here instead, where he could keep an eye on her. And keep an eye out for her.

Being alone together was just one of the fringe benefits of the job. Even the bounty-hunting business had its perks.

He'd wanted to share this with her. All this. The idea of it almost made him laugh.

The shack, he knew, wasn't much, but the wild beauty outside, that was something. It still reminded him of better days, of his younger years when he'd wanted to be up with the sun, off at the first crack of light, exploring everything. Climbing trees in search of hawks' nests. Hunting crayfish down at Plantation Creek. Challenging Rand to a gator-wrestling match.

Almost getting himself eaten in the process. He could still feel the rush of adrenaline as he approached the scaly ten-foot monster with nothing but his boasting and his bare hands. He hadn't had a lot of sense back then, but he'd still had the sense to be scared. And nothing had scared him like that in a very long time.

He wasn't proud of the fact. It wasn't courage, he knew. Courage came from being afraid and doing a job anyway. Bravery came from facing your fear. But he wasn't brave. He was fearless.

He was numb.

Until he'd met her.

Until last night, when she'd been in danger. *That* had terrified him. Bullets, beatings, body piercing, they were all nothing compared to his fear for her safety.

For the first time in a very long while, he'd found something he cared about. Nick Duval. The most passionate, stubborn, difficult, desirable, *repressed* woman he'd ever met. Go figure.

But caring about someone, that could have serious drawbacks for a man in his line of work. He had to stay focused, free, and completely detached to do his job well. He couldn't let himself get soft around the edges. Having a heart, that could lead to trouble.

Serious trouble.

They were both in it this time, he and Nick, together. She didn't know it yet, but Picasso was the least of her problems right now. She was safe from everything here. Everything except her protector.

Sure, he'd brought her here for a purpose. But having her bunched up against him all sexy and sweet and sleep tousled made it hard to remember just what that purpose was. Protection? Protection be damned.

This was survival.

A man and a woman. A secluded hideaway. They could lead to only one thing.

Breakfast.

It was suicidal to think about anything else. He eased himself out of bed to go scrounge up some food, leaving her to sleep the morning off in peace.

Martinique woke to the smell of something wonderful. Something that her painfully empty stomach instantly identified. Food.

It was sizzling in the skillet on the stove, sending fresh, spicy waves of tantalizing, appetizing aromas wafting toward her. Eggs? Onions, peppers? She was so hungry, she wasn't sure it mattered.

She sat up in bed, turning toward the delectable

smells. Cade was at the stove, shirtless, clad only in a pair of faded cutoff shorts, stirring the mouth-watering concoction. A man of many talents, she mused. A provider and a protector. A Cajun and a gentleman. And he could cook too.

She was definitely in love.

Well, at least in serious *like*. But only because she was so incredibly ravenous. She drew in a deep breath, drinking in the amazing scents as they mingled with the fresh summer air.

"Smells like heaven," she said enthusiastically. "When do we eat?"

"Good morning to you too."

"Sorry. Good morning. It's just that I'm *starving*."

"I can see that," he said dryly. "Are you always like this before you've had your first cup of coffee?"

"Usually," she admitted cheerfully. "Adora says I can be a regular swamp monster in the morning. Whatever that means."

He lifted a steaming tin coffeepot off the stove and poured her a cup. "Trust me, sweetness, it's not a compliment. Swamp monsters are seven feet tall, around three hundred and fifty pounds, with a head of long orange hair and wild, deranged eyes." He reached the edge of the bed in two strides and handed her the frothy mug, then took a step back to study her. "And while the description doesn't exactly fit you, I can see *some* resemblance."

"Very amusing," she retorted, and ventured a healthy swallow of the life-giving liquid. Pungent odors permeated her nostrils. Cinnamon, cloves, orange, and sugar. Brandy seared her throat. Brandy? At this hour of the morning?

Although the sensations were far from unpleasant, they were certainly unexpected. She gave an involuntary cough, and it was several seconds before she found her voice again. "Something tells me this isn't your standard cup of Java."

"It's *café brûlant*," he told her. "Good for anything that ails you. Kills it quick."

She gave him a mischievous grin. "Then you should be keeling over at any moment."

The black eyebrows arched. "You'd like that, would you?"

"Well, no," she admitted. "At least not until you finish fixing my breakfast."

He grinned back. "You *are* a monster in the morning. I have a good mind to turn you over my knee and . . ."

Martinique's pulse picked up as the meaning of the words sank in. He'd stopped in mid-sentence, but both of them knew where the thought was leading. To physical contact. She wasn't sure if it was the brandy or the caffeine or the predatory look in Cade's eye that was having the effect on her. But all at once she found it hard to breathe.

Then again, it could be the cloudy roils of black smoke that were curling out of the skillet. "The food!" she called out, anxiously pointing at the stove. "Save it!"

Swearing virulently, Cade whipped around and jerked the cast-iron pan from its fiery burner, grabbing hold of the handle with the help of a kitchen rag. The egg dish inside sizzled and sputtered, but he'd apparently reached it in time. Only the grease had burned.

"Thank goodness," Martinique murmured.

"You should be thankful," he told her. "You almost had blackened omelette for breakfast." He dished the uncharred remains onto two paper plates and handed her one while she still sat in bed. "Eat hearty," he added. "I rode a long way for the ingredients. The nearest mini-mart is miles from here. And this may be your last hot meal for a while. You could be just too dangerous to keep around a kitchen."

"Me?" she asked, incredulous. "Speak for yourself, buster." But she was too interested in tucking down the food to pursue the argument any further. She plumped the pillows on the bed into a backrest, settled against them, and set to work. "Delicious," she murmured between bites. "Fabulous. You should be a chef."

He was in the middle of eating his own meal at the table, but he nodded his acknowledgment, apparently agreeing with her assessment of his talents.

"So, have you ever seen one?" she asked after a large swallow of the *café* concoction. So what if she was swigging brandy at a not-so-advanced hour of the morning? The normal rules didn't seem to apply to this place. Or to him. Couldn't she enjoy herself, just this once, without self-recrimination, without even thinking about it?

"One what?" he asked.

"A swamp monster. The great big guy with the very bad hair. Ever come across one?"

"Sure," he told her, straight-faced.

"What?" she asked, laughing. "You did not!"

He didn't respond, and after a few minutes of the silent treatment and a few more sips of her drink, she finally gave in. "Okay, you did. So, tell me what happened."

He shrugged, half smiling. "Not much. I met him out back of the cabin one morning. He took one look at me and ran away."

"Smart monster," she murmured. "But I don't believe you."

"Suit yourself, angel-face. But there are plenty of legends that started out here in creek country, and some of them are based on reality. Maybe not the monster. But most of the pirate stories are true. Jean Laffite and his band used to hang out here, eluding the authorities, disappearing into the undergrowth. Some of their gold is still said to be buried close by."

"Pirate gold," she breathed. "Too bad *we* can't find it. Have you ever looked?"

"When I was a kid," he told her, smiling at the memory. "My buddy Rand and I used to scour the place on a regular basis. We found a piece of gold chain once, but it was more likely to have come from a store than a ship. And then we grew up. Became cops. Quit believing."

Martinique blinked in surprise, wondering if the alcohol was playing tricks on her mind. "You were a police officer?" she asked.

"Hard to believe, huh? But true. I quit the force after Rand . . . died. I told them what they could do with their bloody rule book. Crooks don't play by the rules. Neither do I. Not anymore."

"Your friend," she said gently, "how did he die? What happened?"

"It was an accident," he said bluntly. "He ran into a bullet."

EIGHT

Martinique gave a soft gasp when she saw the expression in Cade's eyes. It was a look of pure anger and pain, a look so intense, his gaze seemed to be lit by a cold blue fire. He was still suffering from the loss of his friend; he was in agony from his own frustration and fury. And she didn't have any idea how to help him. She only knew that she wanted to. Very, very much.

She was almost afraid to ask for more details. She wasn't sure how Cade would react to her intrusion. But she was more afraid to leave it alone.

"Who shot him?" she finally said, keeping her voice soft.

"I was there," he told her, ignoring her question for the moment. "I watched him die."

Martinique couldn't respond. Her throat was too full, her eyes too close to tears. She could barely even swallow. But she didn't have to speak. After a while Cade continued, talking slowly, deliberately.

"It was a guy we'd busted the week before. Routine stuff. Some minor charge. I can't even remember. But they let him out on bail. And he decided to pay us back. And he succeeded. In a very big way."

"I'm sorry," she whispered, still at a loss to find the right words, the ones that would take some of his ache away. But at the same time, she knew there weren't any. "I'm so sorry."

"It's not your fault, angel-face. It's not anyone's fault. That's what they kept telling me, even Rand's widow, Lori. *It's not anyone's fault.* But someone should've paid for it. The creep didn't pay for it. I brought him back to jail, but it isn't enough to make up for something like that. Nothing is."

"Not even catching other bad guys, maybe stopping them from doing the same thing to somebody else?"

"You mean my career choice?" he asked, letting out a low, bitter laugh. "The police psychologist called it a post-traumatic stress response. Right before I walked out of his office. I prefer to think of it as therapy."

He stood and cleared off the table, signaling that their conversation had come to an end. Martinique didn't attempt to press the matter any further. It was an old wound she'd touched inside Cade, one that hadn't had a chance to heal.

But he'd been willing to share it with her. And she knew instinctively he hadn't opened up like that in a long time. Maybe he'd needed to tell her about his past as much as she'd needed to hear it.

Cade a cop? It was a hard idea to get used to. She'd never imagined him doing something so stable. But for the first time she was beginning to understand how he'd ended up a bounty hunter, always on the road, without any real ties at all. Without any permanent attachments.

Maybe he wasn't as much like Angelé's use-'em-and-lose-'em lovers as she'd first imagined. Not one of them had ever thought of anything or anyone except themselves. But Cade had already saved her from Picasso once, risking his own safety in the process. He hadn't thought of himself, or even the reward. He'd thought of her.

Maybe he really was one of the good guys after all.

"Ready to wash up?" he asked, the low, rusty voice breaking into her reverie, sending her thoughts scattering.

"Wash up?" she asked eagerly. "As in shower?"

He hesitated. "Well, you *could* call it a shower. Come on. I'll show you."

Martinique grabbed the nylon cosmetic pack she'd stowed inside her duffel and followed Cade onto the back porch. Now that her stomach had stopped growling, she couldn't wait to get cleaned up. She was still wearing last night's clothes, khaki slacks and a simple knit shirt, which weren't exactly at their best after she'd slept in them. A wash and a change would be extremely welcome.

He led her outside where a wide, wooden balcony flanked the back of the cabin. The cedar planks were silver with age, the rail along the water's edge somewhat rickety, but Martinique barely noticed. She was too busy drinking in the amazing beauty of the marsh at morning.

There was water everywhere she looked, water and sky and trees and wildness, all melting together in brilliant tones of blue and green. Sunlight dappled along the wet, meandering tributaries, radiant and dazzling in its own reflection. A flock of lazy wood ducks dotted the surface, bobbing languidly in the bottle-green water like plump, painted, clockwork boats. A bald eagle circled overhead, majestic, magnificent in flight.

Martinique felt her heart soaring right along with it. "Oh!" The word escaped her almost involuntarily. "No wonder you have your place here," she said simply. "No wonder."

It did seem to suit him perfectly. He was like one of those pirates. Guarding against any civilized intrusions, a law unto himself, hidden in an impenetrable fortress of gnarled cypress and bog, of green leaves and gray moss bunting. Exiled into seclusion like one of his *l'Acadie* French ancestors.

"Glad you like it here, angel-face."

"I like the surroundings," she said, correcting his assumption with a teasing smile. "The cabin could use some work."

"Uh-oh. You're not going to suggest a fleur-de-lis wallpaper, are you? Or start sewing cute little curtains for the kitchen window?"

"I was thinking more along the lines of a bulldozer," she shot back. "It looks like it's already been decorated. By a band of marauding gypsies."

"Gypsies?" he asked doubtfully.

"Exactly. They took all the good stuff with them."

He pointed to an old metal spigot that was sticking

out of the back wall. Rusted and mossy, it protruded from the cabin piping approximately six feet above porch level. "Everything except for the showerhead," he told her.

Martinique eyed the creaky handle and narrow spout with grim foreboding. "That's it?" she asked. "No soap dish? No towel rack? No *curtain?*"

He folded his arms across his chest, studying her. "You know what your problem is, Nick? You're just too used to all those luxuries."

She narrowed her eyes at him. "My problem? Ha! Now I know why you didn't hesitate to take a dip in my fountain. It's like a pool at the Taj Mahal compared to this."

"You don't have to shower," he said, shrugging. "It's your choice. But remember, there isn't any air-conditioning out here, either. You could get pretty ripe after a few eighty-degree days. I might have to dunk you in the creek by then. Or toss you out of bed. Whichever's easiest."

"Toss me out of . . . ! Don't flatter yourself, Jackson. I had a moment of weakness last night, but you won't find me sharing the same mattress again. I was cold. And scared. I heard noises."

"Believe me, Nick, I wasn't complaining. That's twice now you've ended up in my arms after noises that went bump in the night. Maybe you're feeling things instead of hearing them."

"I'm not feeling anything!" she insisted.

He tucked a hand under her chin and tipped her head back, searching her eyes. "That might be another

one of your problems, Nick. You won't let yourself feel,
even though I know you're capable of it. We're just
gonna have to work on that."

"I don't have any problems!" she exclaimed, backing
up, out of his reach. "But if I did, I suppose you'd be
just the man to help me work on them. Just the man to
bring those feelings out?"

"I might be, *chérie*," he said, sizing up her every
move with those watchful, all-seeing eyes.

But it was that word more than anything that had
her heart melting into warm liquid mush. *Chérie.* Lord,
but she wished he hadn't called her that again. It simply
undid her, that guttural, sexy, Gallic accent of his, the
way his voice stroked her slowly.

It reminded her too vividly of the last time he'd
called her that. And where his hands had been when he
was doing it. Inside her. Everywhere. It was almost as if
it were happening again, as if he were enticing her
slowly, this time with only a word.

"I suppose you've already had your shower?" she
asked, grasping at the first sentence she could think of
that might change the subject. Any topic would be safer
than the one he was touching on right now.

"First thing this morning. But I wouldn't mind another one. What do you say, sweetness? Want some
company?"

"I say no. And you'd better not be watching out of
any back windows while the water's on. I'm . . . shy."

"You could've fooled me."

"Promise, Jackson. No peeking."

He raised his right hand in the air, palm out, and

nodded solemnly. "Scout's honor. But it's going to spoil all the fun."

"This may be asking for too much," she said, "but a towel to dry off with would sure come in handy. Happen to have any?"

"I might be able to dig one up," he told her. "Go ahead and start. I'll toss it out to you." And on those very unreassuring words, he disappeared inside.

Martinique glanced around her, suddenly self-conscious. It was silly, she knew. They were in the middle of nowhere. But she had to check out the scenery several times to convince herself no one was watching. No one except the birds, anyway.

She let out a long sigh, and after another cautious survey of her immediate surroundings, she started to strip. She was all the way down to her bra and panties when her modesty started to kick in again. It was so strange, the idea of exposing herself in the open air and sunshine. The thought of standing outside, naked, in the middle of the day. Especially with Cade so close.

How did she know he wouldn't walk out at any moment and see her? Just the thought of it sent a sharp, terrifying thrill all the way down to her toes. She could imagine the look in his eyes, hungry with need, dark with desire. A terrible, dangerous, heart-stopping look. Would he be angry? Excited? Out of control? Dear Lord, she didn't want him to catch her without her clothes.

Did she?

She closed her eyes, trying to picture his reaction in

her mind, trying to imagine that she was undressing in front of him. Right here. Right now. Just like this.

She reached back, unlatching the hooks on her bra. The lace whispered open, dropped to the deck at her feet. Her breasts flowed free of the garment, full and warm, as a sultry breeze brushed delicately across her skin, tautening her softest, most tender places. Her shyness dropped away as well, to be replaced by something sweeter, less inhibiting.

Sensuality.

She loved the way she felt. Free. Unbound. Bewitching. What *would* Cade do if he saw her like this? What would he say?

"God, but you're beautiful."

Every nerve in Martinique's body was electrified by the sound. The voice was too intense, too gruff and blatantly masculine to have come from her imagination. Too real to be something she'd just made up. Her eyes fluttered open.

Cade stood before her.

She didn't have to imagine his response any longer. It was hot and forbidden, the way he was watching her, shocking her with wave after wave of pure, overpowering sexuality. But she was more shocked by her own response. She didn't try to hide herself, or cover her body in any way. She liked the way he was looking at her. She liked the daring, almost dizzying way it made her feel.

Cade stopped dead in his tracks. It took a supreme, almost superhuman effort, but he checked the primitive impulse to stride forward and take Nick in his arms, to take her right then and there. She was tempting him beyond all reason to go ahead and do it. She was *inviting* him to take a long look at exactly what he'd been missing. Exactly what he'd been needing for all this time.

He'd wanted women before, but it had never been like this. Never this deep, burning drive of desire that only one woman could assuage. Just Nick. Every curving, cresting, carnal inch of her.

She had him in agony.

He hadn't meant to catch her by surprise like this. He hadn't realized she would lose her inhibitions, or her clothes, so quickly. Hell, the water wasn't even running yet. But as soon as he'd stepped through the doorway to bring her a towel, he'd been riveted by the sight of her. By the incredible, bare-breasted, mind-blowing sight.

She was sleekly built, with smooth, flowing, very female lines. No angles anywhere. Just soft, voluptuous body parts, all of them made to pleasure a man. Or make him beg for mercy.

Her breasts were the most perfect he'd ever seen. Not too large, but so sweetly formed, he could imagine them cupped in his hands, or fitted exquisitely against his lips, tender and full as sun-ripe fruit. It made him hard just to look at them, just to picture the dark nipples peaking as he sampled them slowly, wetting the tips with his tongue, taking them into his mouth as he tasted their sensitive surface.

He was the one who needed the shower right now, not her. But he was so explosively hot, so granite hard from the show she was giving him, he doubted it would do any good. Muscles inside him were gripped so tight, emergency surgery couldn't save him at this point.

Nothing could save him. He was a goner unless he could have her. But she wasn't through with his torture yet. She wanted to kill him slowly, it seemed.

She closed her eyes, as if she couldn't quite face what she was about to do herself. Her head fell back as she turned sideways, reached for the faucet, and turned the water on. Cade watched the liquid streaming across her breast, down her shoulder and back, sheening her entire body in cool moisture and steaming sunlight. She still had her panties on, plastered wetly, provocatively across her backside. Parts of her were still too modest, too afraid of him to take that final step.

But the rest of her was just gutsy enough to give him something to gawk at. When she went for the bar of soap and started lathering herself up, Cade felt himself fighting for air. And he finally stopped fighting his nobler instincts.

Whether she understood it or not, Angel-face just wasn't playing fair. Sure, he'd promised not to peek. But it had been an accident, after all.

And if this was her way of making him pay for his impertinence, the price was just too high. He couldn't simply stand by and watch any longer. If she wanted to shower with an audience, she had to expect some audience participation.

He stepped under the stream with her, and took the soap from her hands. "Want me to wash your back?"

Martinique wasn't sure what she wanted just then. Except some merciful sort of relief from the ache she

felt inside. The ache to have Cade with her, all to herself, at least for a little while. The ache to know every
part of him, to feel him inside every part of her.

She hadn't meant for the exhibition to go quite this
far. But she'd been so surprised to see him standing
there, she hadn't had time to stop and think about her
own actions and the consequences they might bring.
For once, she'd let herself go, let herself react totally on
instinct.

Unfortunately, her instincts had gotten completely
out of control. Probably the result of holding herself in
check for so long. For her entire life, in fact.

And she had no idea what to do now.

One more step and there would be no turning back,
for either of them. One more step and she might end up
as heartbroken as Angelé had always been. But on some
deep level she'd wanted to bring them both to this
point. On some level she wanted him to make the decision for her, no questions asked.

To do exactly what he was doing now. Touching her
without waiting for permission. Coaxing her without
stopping to get an answer.

"Turn around for me, Nick," he suggested. "Turn
around so we can do this right."

Next thing she knew, she was nestled against him,
her back fitted firmly to the massive muscles in his
chest, her buttocks pressed to the hard wall of his
thighs. Water trickled around them, between them, cool
and fresh, making Martinique's skin tingle with liquid
anticipation.

But when Cade finally started scrubbing her with

the slippery bar of soap, it wasn't her back he was concentrating on. It was her belly. He was working in slow,
concentric circles around her torso, starting at the upper
edge of her panties and sweeping in a wide arc just beneath her breasts. Always teasing, not quite touching
them.

Lather lapped at her skin, slick and sensual beneath
his skillfully moving hands. A soft moan escaped her.

She heard Cade growl something in response, something low in Cajun French she couldn't quite understand. But at that point she didn't care. She was too busy
concentrating on his hands, wondering at what point
they were actually going to make contact with her achy,
swollen breasts.

He was still teasing with his fingers, still lubricating
her with the soap, circling each mound in turn, advancing toward the taut, overflowing centers and retreating
just when her expectations were at their highest. But as
soon as she was ready to cry out with physical frustration, with the sheer need for the relief of his touch, he
stopped circling, and his hands found the hard, heat-
filled nubs of her nipples.

He rolled them insistently between his fingertips, as
rough skin made gentle friction against soft. He plea-
sured both at the same time, pulling each peak repeatedly, until Martinique's knees started buckling beneath
her. Until she wanted to weep, the sensations were so
intense, so exquisite.

She wasn't sure at what point she did start to actually cry, at what point the salt from her tears mingled

with the water splashing across her face. Or at what point her body began trembling.

She only knew she was incapable of stopping either reaction. And equally incapable of explaining the cause. Whether it was the coolness of the water, or the conflict and frustration inside her, or just an overdose of hormones that had lain dormant for too long, she wasn't sure.

But Cade seemed to understand her feelings this time, even better than she did herself. With only a single harsh groan, he stopped the slow, sweet battering on her defenses and pulled her from beneath the shower, quickly wrapping a towel around her. The same towel that had started all the trouble in the first place.

"Never mind, Nick," he said hoarsely. "Hell, woman, I can't take it if you get all weepy on me. I didn't mean to make you cry."

Martinique wiped her eyes with the edge of the towel, still shaking, trying to get herself back under control. "It's not your fault," she sniffed. "I don't know *what's* wrong with me. I'm not sure I can explain it."

"Try," he pleaded, raking his damp, dripping hair back from his face in frustration. "This whole thing isn't going to work unless I get what's going on with you. Fill me in on the facts, Nick. Just what is it about me, about *us*, you don't want to deal with?"

NINE

It was mid-afternoon before Martinique finally had a chance to explain anything to Cade. Talking didn't come easy when you were still wearing wet panties, with only a towel for a top. Being in a state of full physical arousal hadn't helped much either.

But he hadn't pressed her any further at that point. He'd left her alone to finish her shower in private. To give them both a chance to calm down.

Which she had, sort of. At least being completely dry and fully dressed helped. A little.

Until she found him on the front porch, lying in a comfortable hammock, drowsy and adorable with a dark wave of hair falling across his forehead. He looked too sexy for words, she thought, taking a moment to study him at her own risk. One powerful leg hung over the edge of the rope netting, and he pushed off with it every now and then, swinging himself back and forth in the breeze.

He seemed strangely distant, lying there, his expression far away, full of mystery. She wondered exactly where he was just then, with his eyes focused on the far horizon.

"Want me to make some room?" he asked, clearly more aware of her presence than she'd realized. His senses were so fine-tuned, so sharp and alert, she wondered if it was a skill he'd developed on the job or an inherent sensitivity he'd been born with. Either way, that heat-seeking radar of his was sure getting her into trouble.

"No thanks." She pulled up a painted wooden porch chair. "I'll sit." No way was she going to get horizontal with him in that hammock. Not when it had taken several hours away from him just to get her sanity back. "I appreciate you giving me some space," she added. "I needed it."

"Take all the room you want, Nick," he told her. "No one's crowding you."

She looked off toward the horizon, to where his gaze had been moments before. It was hard to face him with what she had to say. Too hard to look him directly in the eye. "You've been pretty patient with me," she said finally. "I know I owe you an explanation."

"You owe me nothing, Nick. But I'll admit I'm curious. What happened back there, between us, could've been so good. Hell, *nothing* happened and it was still close to a religious experience. Why can't you give it a chance?"

"I think it has something to do with my last name," she said, sighing. "Duval. The women in my family all

had some pretty precarious pasts where men were concerned. There's not a lady in the lot for two hundred
years running. So you see, I'm not what you think."

His long pause seemed like an eternity to her. The
answer that followed was thoughtful and surprising.
"You're wrong about that, Nick. I care a helluva lot
more about you than about what any of your dead relatives did. The woman I think you are hasn't got a thing
to do with your past."

"Maybe. But I can't dismiss it so easily. My mom,
Angelé, she was the biggest mess of them all. She was
a . . . dancer. A Bourbon Street stripper."

It was a relief to say it out loud. To say it to someone
like him. Someone hard and cynical and strong enough
to handle the truth.

When he didn't respond immediately, she had a
sick, sinking feeling in the pit of her stomach, wondering if he really would think less of her, after all. But he
might as well know the whole of it right now. "Men
paid my mother to take her clothes off," she added
bluntly. "That's how she supported us. I hope that
doesn't shock you."

"I'm not shocked," he said finally. "I'm sorry. That's
no kind of life for a little girl."

She shrugged, grateful for the kindness in his voice,
but even more grateful that she hadn't heard a trace of
pity. "I guess my mom did the best she could under the
circumstances. But I swore I would never be like her."

A frown creased the strong, suntanned surface of his
forehead. "Nick, I think I know what you're getting at.
And I'm glad you told me. But you're *not* like her.

You're not like anyone. You deserve a chance to find that out for yourself. To explore your own responses to life."

"I'm not sure I have the courage," she said, meeting those intense blue eyes of his for the first time since their conversation began. "Sometimes when we're together, when we're . . . physical, it scares me."

"What scares you, sweetness?"

"The way I feel. Wonderful. Wicked. Like the Duval legacy is catching up with me. Like I'm just as fallen as the rest of them were. Maybe even *worse.*"

"So what you're saying is, it feels bad when I make you feel good?"

"Silly, huh?"

"*Not* silly, Nick. Understandable. Especially if you've been trying to make up for someone else's past."

She sighed. "It's like carrying around a very heavy, very scandalous history book and trying to rewrite the pages."

Cade nodded, his expression sympathetic. "A long line of notorious relations. That's a lot for one woman to erase all by herself, don't you think? Unless you have the magic power to change the past. Which I don't believe any of us do."

"I know I can't change it," she admitted. "I'm just afraid I'll repeat it."

"Nick," he said patiently, "it's not fair to hold yourself responsible for their mistakes. And what if you did make a few of your own? A little fear, that's natural, even healthy. Fear serves a purpose. It's a survival signal that keeps us safe and cautious in risky situations. It prevents us from getting ourselves killed. But when you're scared to open yourself up—afraid to feel—that's not living."

She eyed him doubtfully. "So you don't see my . . . responsiveness—the way I get out of control with you—as a serious character flaw?"

He smiled at that. "Serious?" he asked. "Hell, yes, it's serious. Seriously exciting. But I haven't gotten you out of control yet, *chérie*. Not yet. I want you ready for that."

Martinique's heart went a little crazy at the promise in his words. She wasn't sure she'd ever be prepared for the experience he had in mind. Could she really let go with a man as frighteningly potent, as dangerously male as Cade? Did she dare let her guard down with him again, for certain this time?

"Maybe we could take it gradually," she suggested, a little shaky, still unsure. "One step at a time."

"Take it slower?" he asked, apparently assessing that possibility for the very first time. Cade Jackson had probably never done anything at a regular pace his entire life. "Now there's a concept. Tell you what, sweetness, why don't we get out of here for a while? Go someplace public where I *have* to keep my hands off you. More or less."

"Like a date?" she asked.

"Like a night on the town. I happen to know a little honky-tonk hangout nearby where the music—"

"Just give me half an hour to get ready."

"Eager to go, are you?"

Eager to save herself was more like it. It didn't matter where they went as long as it was away from this very disturbing little shack. A private honeymoon suite at the Hilton couldn't be more secluded, more sexually uninhibiting as this Shangri-la on stilts. Putting space between them and it was just what she needed right now.

"I can't wait," she told him. "I've never been to a honky-tonk. What should I wear?"

"Clothes," he said, deadly serious. "Lots of them. Or I might just forget about the bargain we made."

Simple jeans and a silky, sleeveless blouse were what Martinique finally settled on wearing. Not that she had a whole lot of wardrobe to choose from, considering the very limited size of her suitcase. But something about the idea of a *date*, with Cade, had stirred her Cinderella instincts. So, maybe they weren't exactly going to a ball, but she'd been to enough stuffy affairs to know that gala evenings weren't necessarily the most exciting that life had to offer.

A honky-tonk, with *him*. Now that could be some serious fun. Something she hadn't let herself have in a long time. Something she'd never had much of, not even as a child.

Angelé's dingy apartment had been too full of reality to afford the young Martinique much opportunity for playtime. As an adult, she'd spent most of her time just surviving, throwing herself into the business, trying to build some sort of security for herself. But tonight that struggle could be forgotten for a while, set aside for an evening out. Tonight there was something in the air, some stirring inside her that said it was okay to feel the magic, just this once . . .

Propping the mirror from her purse open on the wooden table, she swept mascara across her dark lashes, glossed her lips with a glorious shade of orchid, and tied her hair on top of her head in a wavy, curling cascade. She wondered for a second just who the woman staring back at her really was. Someone . . . sexy. Desirable. Someone she didn't immediately recognize. A woman she just might want to get to know better.

A woman who strolled into the honky-tonk with Cade that evening, every nerve inside her fairly buzzing in anticipation. She was awash with energy, but without a clear idea of what to expect from anything. From the night, or the man with her. Least of all, from herself.

The hangout he'd brought her to held the first surprise. It was packed and rowdy, all right, almost raucous in the amount of music and merrymaking that floated up to the rough-hewn log rafters, but it wasn't the least bit sleazy. No ten-dollar tramps dressed in tight rubber outfits. Just a whole lot of locals having an all-out good time.

Holding her by the hand, a gesture Martinique secretly found at once old-fashioned and hopelessly romantic, Cade made a spot for them at the bar, under a beat-up sign reading *Ici on parle français*. He ordered their drinks in fluent French, two icy mugs of frosty, locally brewed beer.

"*À ta santé*," he said, handing her a glass, clinking

the mugs together in casual unison. "*Laissez les bon temps rouler.*"

"Amen to that," she responded. "Let the good times roll."

The *bière* was dark and delicious, probably aged forever in special wooden casks that gave it the elusive, lagerlike flavor. Martinique turned to watch the dance floor, filled with dressed-down revelers waltzing wildly in a circle to the *chank-a-chank* sound of the Cajun country band. The beat was so compelling, it was nearly impossible not to move in time to the music. She felt her hips swaying almost involuntarily.

"Come on, sweetness." Cade stored their beers on the bar and whisked her out onto the floor. "Let's work off a little of our excess energy together."

Martinique decided it was an altogether excellent idea. A little physical exertion was what they both needed to cope with the incredible tension that had been building all day. Ever since they'd met, in fact. Willingly, she let herself get carried away by Cade and the insistent sound of the crazy music.

Unfortunately, dancing together didn't do much to calm either of them down. In fact, it had exactly the opposite effect. Friction, Martinique decided, was a large part of the problem.

She could feel it every time she moved, in every back-and-forth, up-and-down, side-by-side beat. The up-close, confident way Cade held her didn't lessen the impact any. His hand tightened on the small of her back as their hips locked together, swiveling and circling in seductive unison.

· It was mad, Martinique decided, rotating pelvis to pelvis in such an incredibly public place. Cajun waltzing didn't begin to describe the quick, abandoned motions they were making with their bodies. Dirty dancing, that's what it was. Making love, upright.

Fully clothed, of course. And while nobody in the room seemed to mind, it was probably illegal in most southern states. They were very likely about to be arrested any second now, but Martinique was past the point of caring. She couldn't believe *she* was the one doing it. She couldn't believe how much fun she was having.

"Nice moves, Nick," Cade whispered in her ear.

She felt a sharp thrill of pleasure at the approval in his words, understanding that nice had nothing to do with the way either of them were dancing. The moves Cade was putting on her were so skillful, so erotic and audacious, they were downright decadent.

His eyes were full of meaning when he looked at her, blue-hot and sinfully beautiful. Martinique couldn't do a thing except stare right back. She could feel the sharp tug of his interest shooting right through her, sending a sweet shock of vibrancy straight to the soles of her feet. His fingers were tensing and releasing on the tender notch in her back, slowly massaging at the very base of her spine in a way that made her muscles melt. There was a languorousness washing over her, a delicious weakness flooding through her veins.

And still he stared into her eyes, searching her face, mesmerizing her with that knowing, sensual smile. *I know what you want*, his expression said. *I know what you need.*

Her heart nearly came to a stop as he continued to press her closer, mastering her mind with the look in his eyes as his hands mastered the rest of her. The Cajun music crashed around them, hot and heavy, throbbing to the current of excitement that was pulsing in her throat. But just as the room was getting revved up, the sounds and stomping going at full tilt, the rhythm eased into something infinitely slower.

The lights went down. Cade cuddled her full up against him. And suddenly Martinique realized she was lost.

She didn't even try to pretend otherwise. She was through with pretending. She was done for.

His hand slipped even lower in the darkness, palming at the base of her bottom, making her far more aware of the sweet ache that was welling up inside her. Making her more aware of *him*, and parts of him that were growing harder by the minute. It hadn't worked, that ingenious idea of his about going to a safe public place. Because here they were, in the middle of a shadowed crowd, and things were still happening between them.

Thrilling, shocking, irresistible things.

She wasn't sure she could fight her feelings for him any longer. She wasn't sure she wanted to. This longing she felt to be with him went far beyond the physical. It had to do with the kind of man he was. The kind of man he'd proved himself to be.

Primitive, passionate. A protector. He could be cruel

when it came to chasing crooks, but incredibly caring when it came to looking after her. He could be brave and reckless, having his belly button pierced to pursue Picasso, but infinitely patient and understanding with her.

She knew, somewhere deep in her soul, that Cade Jackson could never be a permanent part of her life. He was too much a wild, lone drifter ever to settle down and be the stable, family man she'd always imagined herself with. Just seeing that barely civilized shack of his was enough to show her they would never want the same things. A home would always be of paramount importance to her, but it was obviously at the bottom of his list.

So why did his crude little cabin still seem like the most amazingly romantic place she'd ever been to? Why was she standing here, holding on to him so hard, longing for something that couldn't possibly last? Wanting to have him, if only for a while.

"Take me home," she whispered in his ear, urgent.

Cade felt his body go still at the sound, almost frozen in motion. "What?" he asked, half in shock, hoping to confirm that he'd heard right. Hoping it meant what he thought it did. *Praying* it meant just that.

"Take me home," she repeated, a bit shyer this time, but still sounding earnest. "Take me home and make love to me."

Cade felt his gut clenching tight at her words, muscles contracting into an advanced, aching state of anticipation. She'd meant it, all right. She couldn't have said it much clearer. But did she really know what she was getting herself into?

He tipped her head back, forcing her to look at him. It was pressing his luck, he knew, but some part of him just had to ask. "You sure about this, sweetness?"

She let out a long, shaky sigh. A sigh of surrender. The unmistakable expiration of a woman in the throes of pure physical need. Just the sound of it arced through him like a lightning bolt between the legs, jolting him beyond belief. Lord, but she was sexy when she went all soft on him like that.

"Very sure." She blinked at him with those innocent, incredible eyes.

Sure, *she* was sure. But *he* didn't know if he could wait until he got her home.

"Whatever you say, *chérie*," he told her. "Whatever you want. Just give me two minutes to take care of something first. I need to get a message back to the city."

Cade couldn't believe he was thinking about business at a time like this. He couldn't believe he'd even remembered his master plan at such a moment. But after all, the deal he wanted to make had a lot to do with Nick. Hell, it had everything to do with her.

If it worked, it would secure her safety and peace of mind. He only hoped it *would* work. He only hoped Picasso would take the bait he intended to offer.

"A message?" she asked, softly, sweetly.

Clearly Nick's mind was *not* on business. He was grateful for that. Grateful he hadn't completely distracted her from matters of a more immediate nature.

Business was one thing. But whatever happened tonight would be very, very personal.

"A quick one," he promised. "A short fax I want to send. This place has the only machine available for miles."

"I'll wait," she told him. "Over there by the door. Okay?"

Was it okay for her to wait for him? Lord, anything Nick wanted to do was fine in his book as long as it involved the two of them leaving together shortly. After reassuring her that her plan was perfect, he took off to dispatch the fax at shotgun speed.

Luckily, the club manager was downright cooperative with Cade's request. A twenty-dollar bill got him an invitation to the back office and easy access to the miracles of modern technology. Minutes later the note was on its way to the fence's French Quarter location.

And Cade was driving Nick back to his place as fast as his bike would carry them. After what seemed like an eternity, they were finally inside the shack again. Amazingly enough, she still hadn't changed her mind.

"This is really what you want?" he asked again, like a complete blithering idiot.

He could have kicked himself for it, for laughing in the face of his miraculous good fortune, but he still wanted to give her a chance to back out. She was so vulnerable, he knew. He hadn't brought her to his home to ravish her. And yet that was exactly what he was about to do.

Ravish her beyond both their wildest dreams.

But he didn't think he could handle it if she got hurt

somehow in the process. He had to know that she was going into this with her eyes wide open.

"It really is," she reassured him, then hesitated. "Don't you want to anymore?"

Cade couldn't wait to reassure her right back and show her just how bad he wanted this to happen between them. But he wasn't going to frighten her with his own physical urgency this time. He was going to make it sweet for her. Sweeter than magnolia honey. Hotter than Acadian cayenne.

"Oh yes," he said roughly, reaching behind her, pulling the pins from her hair. He watched, fascinated, as it fell to her shoulders in soft, smoldering waves. "I *do* want to."

Moonlight shimmered through the cabin windows, sparkling her hair with silver fire. Her eyes were alight with it, too, the irises brimming like twin pools of liquid heat. She didn't seem quite real standing there, so iridescent and ethereal, and yet so willing, so close. But he knew she was real. His body was telling him in the most immediate, most overpowering way.

Muscles tightened as a mass of energy spilled toward his groin. One look at Nick and he needed her. All to himself. In ways he was just beginning to imagine.

He was just deciding which way it was going to be tonight when she reached toward him. Her fingers fluttered over the hardness in his jeans, exploring exquisitely. Pleasure slammed through him with so much force, it was almost pain. So much for staying in complete control. It seemed that Nick had other things in mind for him.

She worked the zipper on his pants down slowly, freeing the hardest part of him with trembling, tentative hands. He heard himself groan when her fingertips finally made contact. One experimental stroke and she had him in sweet agony.

"Don't do that," he warned, catching her wrists and pulling both hands behind her.

"Oh!" she breathed, embarrassed. "You don't like it?"

Did he *like* it? Didn't she understand it was sending him into cardiac arrest? She was so full of contrasts, so blatantly sensual and at the same time such an innocent. No, he decided, she couldn't be *that* innocent. She had to know she'd already reduced him to a hopeless case with that mind-blowing butterfly touch. He was half-crazed already and they'd barely even started.

"What I would *like*," he told her, carrying her over to the table and seating her on top of it, "is for you to put those incredible hands of yours to different use." He spread her arms on either side of him, planting both sets of fingertips firmly against the table edge. "Now hold on tight, sweetness. Hold on and don't let go until the universe explodes."

Which is exactly what he wanted to happen for her. And he knew exactly how to go about it. Cajun style. Spicy-hot and sizzling.

He popped open the top button of her jeans, testing. She gave a soft, shocked gasp. The sound of her excitement sent his pulse skyrocketing. But her hands didn't stray. They were still wedged against the tabletop, a little whiter now, a little shaky, but hanging on all the same.

"Good, *chérie*," he whispered. "You're doing fine. Just don't let go."

He inched her zipper down slowly, teasing her a little at a time, the same way she'd done to him. A tremor of anticipation shook her shoulders. Her head fell back, her body arching as he slipped his hand inside. And stroked her until beads of perspiration broke out along her temples.

She whimpered, shutting her eyes tight, and Cade kissed each eyelid in succession. Unbuttoning her blouse with his free hand, he stripped the lace from her breasts and kissed her there too.

"Cade." She whispered his name hoarsely, like a slow, sweet country song against her lips. "I don't think I can take it."

"Uh-uh," he said, still pleasuring her down below, still petting and caressing slowly. "Not yet, Nick. Hang on for me, just a while longer."

Her arms were shaking now, her whole body trembling from his touch, but Cade still wanted to please her more. He bent to take her breast in his mouth, suckling and sipping at her nipple, drinking in that intoxicating, tender part of her. She gave a soft moan, her voice husky, full of heat.

He knew she was ready for him. She was more than ready. She was slick and wet with wanting. Her hands finally released the table, twining wildly, wantonly through his hair.

Cade caught her against him and carried her over to

the bed, slipping her shoes off, discarding her pants as he settled her down on the sheets. His own clothes followed, falling to a pile on the floor. She gazed up at him, gasping softly as he stood before her naked, revealing the magnitude of his arousal.

Her sweet, sudden shyness as she looked away brought him amazing pleasure. *She* was responsible for all that raging, rampant hardness. She finally understood exactly what she'd done to him. She finally understood what he was about to do to her.

He found his wallet in the pile of discarded clothes, tore open the foil packet he kept inside, and sheathed himself in the condom. "Take your panties off, Nick," he told her. "It's time."

He might have done it for her himself, but he wanted this final gesture to be hers. He needed to know he had her unconditional consent. Sweetly, very sweetly, she complied, removing the last barrier between them with gently trembling hands. The innocent striptease was all the encouragement he needed.

He was ready to take her at that instant. God, if he didn't take her now, he knew he was going to die. He opened her legs, positioning himself at her sweetest, most incredibly private part. He started to impale himself in her softness. And stopped suddenly when he touched tight, tender resistance.

He exhaled slowly, fighting to keep control. Emotions warred for dominance within him, male hormones raging at their highest. His strongest impulse was to keep on pushing, to break through the barrier and make the wildest, most unrestrained, awesome love of his life.

But the unexpected discovery he'd just made had sent his brain into a paralytic state of shock.

The obstacle he'd met could mean only one thing. Angel-face was even more innocent than he'd imagined. She was a *virgin*, for Chrissake. An untouched woman in sensual, seductive disguise.

He swore hoarsely, pulling himself out with supreme effort, with tripwire self-control. "Sweetness," he groaned, aching uncontrollably from the flaring need he felt, "why didn't you tell me this is your first time?"

"I *couldn't*," she said on a tremor, her voice still full of her own hurting need. "I didn't know how to tell you. I didn't know when."

Cade's heart went recklessly weak. He'd had plenty of women before, but never one as completely untried and perfectly trusting as Nick. Never one who was willing to give him such an incredible, irreplaceable gift. Gloriously, wonderfully willing. The only problem was, he didn't know whether or not he should accept it.

He *wanted* to. He wanted to so much, his whole body was begging him to go ahead and give in to the sheer, overwhelming urge of instinct. But a more rational, compassionate part of his brain was warning him to stop.

Making love with a passionate, incredible woman was one thing. Deflowering a defenseless angel-faced virgin was another.

"It doesn't matter, does it?" she asked him. "Please don't stop. I still want to. Even if it hurts."

Cade's heart swelled into his throat, almost choking him. He couldn't handle that he would be the first for

Nick. He couldn't handle the fact that she wanted him to be. What had he done to deserve her?

God, he hadn't even gone easy on her. The sexual tactics he'd used had been pretty advanced from the start. If he'd only known just how vulnerable she was, just how inexperienced with men like him, with *any* men for that matter, he'd never have pushed her so hard.

Hell yes, it mattered. It mattered to him, anyway. Because he knew it mattered to her.

But doing the right thing didn't necessarily make it any easier. It took everything he had to sit up in bed and plant both feet on the floor. Everything and more. God, but she was gorgeous, lying there waiting for him. He pulled the covers up over her, trying to save his own sanity. Or what was left of it, anyway.

"We can't do it, Nick," he told her, hardly believing the words that were coming from his own lips. "Not now. Maybe not ever."

TEN

The instant Martinique woke in the morning, she knew she was alone. Cade's note, tacked on the wall with a kitchen knife, told her the whole, horrifying story.

Sweetness, it said. *Tired of being patient with Picasso. Going back to end this one way or another. Stay put. I promise to return tonight.*

Martinique read and reread the roughly scribbled words several times, trying to make out their cryptic meaning. Clearly, Cade had gone back to the city to track down the creep once and for all. But just what was he planning to do?

Whatever he intended, it had to be dangerous. Cade wasn't exactly the cautious type. He was far too daring, too ready to tempt fate for his own good.

He might get hurt again.

What if he *did* get hurt again? She wouldn't be there to help this time and pull his beautiful, wounded body out of the street. This time, if something happened to him, he might not come back.

He might die.

Just the thought of it sent Martinique's heart sinking all the way down to her stomach. The thought of not seeing him again. The thought of never being with him in the way she'd wanted to the night before.

Lord, how she'd wanted to.

The need for him was still sizzling, warm and bittersweet inside her. She'd done her best to seduce him. She'd been brazen, reaching for him, touching him so shamelessly, she'd shocked them both. Just the memory of it left her cheeks burning.

He'd come so close to taking her. So close to taking what she'd wanted to give. It had to have been agony for him to pull away at that point. It had to have cost him dearly. And yet he'd done it. He'd stopped as soon as he'd discovered it would be her first time.

Why?

Didn't he want her? Was virginity a turnoff to an experienced man like him?

She'd thought he'd wanted to make love, maybe even more than she did. She'd never seen a man in such an advanced state of arousal. She'd never fully understood the effect of testosterone until she'd seen Cade, completely naked and completely erect. The idea of having so much of him inside her had been both terrifying and terribly exciting.

But it hadn't happened. They hadn't even slept in the same bed. Cade had stretched out on the floor with a pillow, apparently loathing the idea of any further physical contact. Had she done something wrong? Made some mistake peculiar to uninitiated maidens?

She didn't *think* so. But then again, she was too inexperienced to know for sure.

Afterward Cade had made no attempt to talk about it. He'd simply made his decision, sacked out, and fallen asleep with exasperating ease. Were all men so good at shifting gears, or was it just this particular man that had the annoying talent?

While he'd seemed to take the episode in stride, she'd lain awake half the night worrying about it, analyzing what had gone wrong. Even in the clear light of day she wasn't sure why it had happened. Or, more accurately, why it hadn't.

He'd been afraid to hurt her, she knew. Afraid of just how close their coupling would bring them. Was that the reason he'd pulled away? If so, he'd sacrificed his own physical gratification because of it.

Or was she simply trying to rationalize his behavior to hide her own feelings of rejection? To avoid the idea that maybe she just wasn't enough woman for him? If that was the case, she'd rather remain mercifully ignorant.

But still, he hadn't taken her just for the sake of his own pleasure. Didn't that prove she'd made the right choice? Didn't that prove just how different he was than Angelé's fast, fly-away lovers? Now, more then ever, Martinique wished they *had* made love.

Now she might never have another chance to convince him just how right it was. It might already be too late to tell him how she felt.

To tell him she was in love with him.

The realization swept over her, welling up inside until it filled her soul completely. At that moment she knew, she *knew* she had to go to him. Because she wanted him to know. Before he had a chance to do something stupid.

She was showered and dressed in seconds flat. Getting transportation back to town, that could be a little tricky. She remembered Cade saying something about a truck, and after a few minutes of hunting around, she located a spare set of keys.

But how to get to the truck? Had he taken the boat himself? She ran out onto the balcony, scanning the shoreline. It wasn't there.

Looking down at the water below, she saw the little canoe, still moored to one of the stilts. Had he waded to shore, not wanting to strand her completely? Had he walked through slimy, knee-deep gator bog just for her sake? Lord, she *did* love him. Never more than at this moment.

Grabbing her purse and duffel, she climbed down into the boat and paddled to shore. She had a moment's scare when she thought the truck might not start, but the engine turned over on the third try. The ride back to town took so long, it seemed almost interminable. It was nearly noon when she pulled up outside her shop again.

Cade's first stop in town was a revisit to the art fence. He didn't lay over there long, just greased the guy's palm enough to get the needed information. Yeah, Picasso had relayed back a response. As soon as Cade heard it, he smiled.

And knew that the plan was going to work.

As long as his luck held out. As long as he stuck to the survival rules. And with Nick stashed safely away, he didn't foresee any further distractions this time. This time he intended to win.

And Picasso was going to help him do it.

Cade could hardly wait to call his bluff. The deal he'd offered was a decoy, but the big-time art thief had agreed to it anyway. On the surface, that is. Underneath, his answer was simple to read. So simple, it was almost transparent.

He'd agreed to meet Cade at Martinique's shop at noon. Consented to it too easily as far as Cade was concerned. Picasso was sadistic, but he wasn't stupid.

The terms had been straightforward enough. If Picasso agreed to bring the paintings back *and* leave Nick alone, Cade promised not to pursue him anymore. He'd lay off the trail for good, let the creep go. Give up his own reward.

Of course, the idea of letting Picasso walk without punishment had made Cade sick from the start. But he'd been prepared to honor even that part of the deal if it really came down to it. If he kept his word, he wouldn't have to bluff. That was the trickiest part about the whole thing. He had to *mean* it, to make it work.

And he did. For Martinique's sake, for her safety, he would have offered almost anything.

If he could get her paintings back in the process, so

much the better. He doubted they were worth much to Picasso anymore. They were just too public at this point to be anything but a tough sell.

But he doubted even more that Picasso was sincerely willing to make the deal. The man had too much ego to take the easy way out. Too much anger not to seek his own sort of revenge.

Martinique had been right when she'd said Picasso wanted to hurt them. But there was no way in hell Cade would let him close to Nick again. Today he would offer himself as bait instead.

And the odds looked pretty good that the big fish was going to bite. Picasso probably would come after him. He'd meet him at the shop, all right. More likely to try to do him in than to make the deal.

But Cade really didn't care why the perp showed up, as long as he showed. As long as he got the chance for the final showdown.

In the meantime a long stop at Killer's was definitely in order. The night before with Nick, well, the night before *almost* with her, had left him with a whole lot of excess energy. Energy he needed to work off.

It was a hopeless cause, he knew. Nothing could ever get her completely out of his system. But he had to try. He *had* to try. Just one more time . . .

Martinique wasn't sure what she'd been expecting to find back at home. It was nearly noon on Sunday, and of course her shop was closed. But she'd given Cade his own set of keys to the place, and the possibility hadn't seemed too remote that she just might meet up with him there. Unfortunately, he wasn't anywhere in sight.

Wondering what to do next, she started to unlock the front door of her store.

And met up with Picasso instead.

"Inside," he ground out, flashing a knife in front of her eyes, then thrusting the point at the base of her back. "Hurry."

Martinique knew he'd left her little choice. She could comply or be killed. And never before in her twenty-eight years had she wanted so much to live.

Quietly, carefully, she led Picasso into the shop. When the door shut behind them, she had a sudden, overpowering sense of déjà vu. It was as if the robbery were happening all over again. Only this time her reaction was vastly different.

This time she couldn't care less what he took. The paintings, the antiques, even the little house she'd always imagined herself working for, they all meant nothing to her at the moment. *Nothing*.

The only thing that mattered was the thought of seeing Cade again. The thought of telling him how much she cared. God, she didn't want to die before she had a chance to do that.

"Don't kill me," she whispered. *"Please,* don't kill me. I'll do anything you want."

"I'll just bet you will, baby," he taunted. "Trouble is, we don't have too much time before your boyfriend arrives. He's meeting me here at noon. Wants to make a deal."

Martinique's heart leaped in her throat. Cade was on

his way! But would he make it in time? Would *he* be the one to get hurt, trying to defend her? She forced herself to keep talking, to gain as much information as possible.

"What—what kind of a deal?"

"Aw, come *on*, baby, don't pretend you didn't know. He's taking the easy way out. I give the paintings back, he gets off my back. But I'm not going to take it. I'm going to take him, instead. Might be fun to sign my name in cowboy blood."

Martinique swallowed hard, fighting back the overwhelming wave of nausea she felt. Picasso was still wielding the knife in his right hand while his free hand began to stroke her. His fingertips traveled across her neck and shoulders, grasping, fondling at her bare flesh until the hair on the back of her neck stood on end. Until her skin crawled from his clammy, insinuating caress.

Revulsion swept over her at the sight of his stringy, unwashed hair, at the faint, sweaty stench of him, at the look of cold, uncompassionate laughter in his clouded black eyes. She knew at that moment she didn't want Cade to show up. She was praying he *wouldn't* show up. Because the expression on Picasso's face told her he would stop at nothing. And she didn't think she could handle it if Cade got himself hurt trying to save her.

"I'll make you a better deal," she blurted out, forcing the words from somewhere deep inside her. "You keep the paintings and leave. Just get out, now, and they're yours."

"Too late, baby," he breathed, twining his long greasy fingers in the loose strands of her hair. "Your art's worthless to me now. You got the word around too good about how hot those paintings are. No one wants to touch them."

He slid his arm around the back of her neck and wrenched her hard up against him. "But I think you got somethin' better to trade. Something your boyfriend probably won't wanna share. So you're gonna give it to me quick, before he gets here."

Martinique felt the bile rising in her throat as his arms locked around her and his thick, sneering lips descended toward hers. But just as the hot stench of his breath was full on her face, she glimpsed the tall shadow of a figure standing directly outside her shop. The figure of a man poised for action.

Cade!

He burst through the door before Picasso could see him coming. The floors of the shop shook from the force. Glass went flying. And Cade drew his gun, leveling it less than four feet from Picasso's head.

"Drop the knife or die," he ground out.

Martinique felt a sharp jerk as Picasso pulled her directly in front of him, using her body as a shield for his.

Cade swore virulently. "Do it, man. Drop your weapon *now*."

"Go ahead," Picasso taunted. "Shoot. But don't forget, I'm an artist with a blade like this. I can do a lot of damage to her before I drop." He brought the knife around to where they all could see it, flicking the steel edge back and forth between Martinique's breasts. "You won't recognize her when I'm done. You won't even want to."

Martinique closed her eyes momentarily, unable to face the agony she read in Cade's eyes. He was furious, she knew. Furious and frustrated and afraid for her. And she didn't know how to help him, or herself. The situation seemed hopeless.

She heard his voice then, bold and brash, cutting through the darkness. "An artist?" he asked Picasso skeptically. "Man, you're an *amateur*."

Picasso's grip on her tightened in anger. The tip of his blade slashed her blouse open, baring the lace of her bra. "Think I don't know what I'm doing? Does *this* look like sloppy work?" He drew blood then, slicing a tiny X in her skin, cutting the surface so quickly, Martinique did little more than wince. Two crimson drops seeped down below her sternum, disappearing inside her shirt.

Cade's face went nearly white with fury, but he was too fast on his feet to let Picasso read him. He gave his shoulders a careless shrug, let out a cocky laugh. "Sure," he said, "You're good on a woman. But what kind of challenge is that? Women are soft. They're easy. You'll have to show me something else. Show me you can fight like a man. Man to man."

"Drop your gun," Picasso spat out, seething from the insult, "and I will."

"Get real," Cade responded. "Not on your life. But I'm willing to trade. This gun for that." He pointed to an ancient instrument that hung on the wall, an eighteenth-century dueling dagger, pearl handled, with a double-edged silver blade. It was mounted on a simple silk pad, creatively displayed inside a gilded frame. Decorative but deadly.

"Deal," Picasso agreed. "But *she's* going to reach for it. Don't try any tricks."

Martinique complied, taking a step toward the wall with Picasso's knife still pointed at her chest. She ripped the dagger from its resting place and slid it across the floor to Cade.

"Perfect." He picked it up, dropping the gun in its place. "It's an even match." He tested the weight of the handle, tossing it expertly between his hands. "Now we'll see which one of us is the real artist."

Picasso couldn't seem to resist the challenge. He pushed Martinique aside and assumed the stance of a street fighter, focusing all of his attention on Cade. "Get ready to bleed, Cowboy. Get ready to die."

Cade cut the air in front of him with a sharp, intimidating slash. "Better control that temper," he suggested with a patient smile. "It's going to get you into trouble."

Incited to action, Picasso lunged forward. Cade quickly dodged left, avoiding the jab. He gave an insolent grin, goading his enemy on. "Is that the best you can do?"

Picasso let out a low growl, his nostrils flaring, his expression red, enraged.

Martinique stood back as they circled the small room, bodies bent, arms out, eyes locked in mortal concentration. It was a riveting sight, awful and terrifying. She was frozen with fascination, entranced by the horror of it, unable to tear her gaze away from the two men.

Cade feinted to the right, drawing Picasso's aim to one side as he struck from the other, lightning fast. Metal hit flesh. A red stain spread across his opponent's sleeve.

"Careful," Cade cautioned him, solicitous. "Try not to drip on the rug."

Picasso flailed his arms in fury, slashing wildly. It was a desperate move, but he did manage to score a direct hit.

Cade's face was cut.

The wound was jagged, jutting across his cheekbone in a two-inch trail. He wiped it with his arm, directing the blood away from his eye. "Nice effort," he said, his voice still smooth, his tone still calm, coolly teasing. "But you lack technique. Care for a demonstration?"

But he wasn't waiting for an answer. The blow he directed came so fast, Picasso barely had a chance to blink. It was a blow from Cade's boot, a kick so hard, it knocked the knife from his opponent's hand.

Picasso was disarmed, dazed by what had happened. He'd been so busy watching Cade's hands, the strike from below had taken him totally by surprise.

The next thing Martinique knew, the creep was hoisted off his feet, dangled dangerously for a moment in midair, then dropped to the floor with a furious thud. Cade held the dagger between his teeth as he pushed Picasso face down on the ground, snapping handcuffs securely around his wrists.

"Aw, come on, man," Picasso pleaded. "What about our deal?"

From the dark fury Martinique read on Cade's face, she knew Picasso should be grateful he wasn't a dead man by now. He was lucky that the dagger Cade unclenched from his mouth didn't get buried somewhere in *him*. But Cade simply dropped it on the nearest table, then rolled Picasso onto his back with the toe of his boot. "Where are the paintings?" he asked, lethally polite.

Picasso's dark eyes gleamed with some final, frustrated remnant of hope. "You gonna let me go if I tell you?"

Retrieving his gun from the spot where he'd left it, Cade cocked the hammer back and pointed it at his reluctant prisoner. "Tell me and I *might* let you live."

"Don't shoot, man!" Picasso groaned. "They're in a public locker down at the train station. Key's in my pocket."

"Good," Cade responded, apparently satisfied. "You can give the evidence to the authorities. Now, get up. You're finally going to jail."

Cade turned to Martinique then, with a look of watchful concern. "Sweetness, you okay? Think you can hold down the fort until I get back?"

She nodded, so relieved she could barely speak. But she wanted to be strong for him. She *would* be strong for him. She folded her arms across her chest and sent him a grateful smile. "I'll be waiting."

"I'm sorry to call you in on a Sunday afternoon," Martinique apologized, ushering Adora into her bedroom, "but one of your house calls might be the only thing that can save me now."

Adora's eyes grew wide with amazement, then dark with mystery as Martinique explained what she wanted.

"Passion powder?" Adora repeated, shaking her regal, turban-wrapped head. A mass of jeweled charms hung from each earlobe, jingling melodiously as she moved. It was a soothing sound, soft and calming, but her voice was cautious when she spoke. "That's powerful stuff, Nikki. Real powerful."

Martinique took the older woman's strong, richly textured hands in her smaller ones and squeezed hard. "I know. I think I'm ready for it. I *know* I'm finally ready for it. I just have to convince him. Can you help me?"

Adora brought one of Martinique's hands to her cheek and held it there, rubbing gently, the way a loving parent might have. "You know I'll help you, Nikki. If that Cajun cowboy is really the one you want."

Martinique's eyes went warm with the thought of him. "When you get to know him," she said, "you'll love him too."

"Humph!" Adora grumbled. "If you say so."

Martinique smiled. "He's the best, bravest man I ever met. I trust him with my life. Now I'm going to trust him with my love."

Adora's eyes grew warm then, too, and she threw herself into the project with unrestrained spirit. Reaching into her traveling medicine bag, murmuring weird, incoherent words, she pulled out all manner of strange and wonderful potions and proceeded to turn Martinique's bedroom into a mystical, marvelous Eden.

Sweet herbs were strewn across the floor, enriching the sensations of all who entered. Tall clusters of tapering candles were arranged, carefully chosen for their heady scents and vibrant colors. The bed itself was purified with a perfumed elixir as the essence of soft spices and wild roses wafted across the satin sheets. Even Ming and Ching got into the act, padding and strutting as they followed their noses around the room, thoroughly inspecting and inhaling everything.

With Adora's preparations for the enchanted chamber complete, she turned to Martinique at last, holding out a tiny golden vial in her hand. "Two drops," she said solemnly, "behind each ear. No man can resist."

Clasping the slender tube tightly, Martinique gave her a parting hug. "Wish me luck," she whispered.

"I will," Adora answered, still shaking her head doubtfully on her way out of the room. "Believe me, Nikki, I will."

Martinique watched her leave with a mixture of gratitude and excitement. She would be alone with Cade again soon. Very soon, she hoped. But there wasn't much time left to get ready for his return.

A hot shower was definitely in order. A luxurious, relaxing, completely *private* hot shower.

Ten minutes later she stepped out from under the jets, with every inch of her skin marvelously warm and sensually steaming. Reveling in the simple pleasure of her own body, she combed her hair, thoroughly toweled off, and completed the ritual with a light application of sleek, perfumed lotion. Still savoring the way it felt against her soft, naked skin, she slipped on a cool white cotton robe and made her way back to her bedroom.

And met Cade halfway down the hall.

Her breath caught. He looked so rugged standing there, so rough and strong and incredibly handsome, it almost hurt. She wanted him so much at that moment. So much, she only hoped she'd be able to show it.

She remembered how he'd saved her earlier, how he'd put himself on the line for her sake. He'd been willing to fight for her, to risk everything. And even after he'd won, even after the reward was already his, he'd still been determined to get her paintings back. How unimportant those paintings seemed to her now. How important *he'd* become to her in such a short time.

"You—you're back," she managed to stammer. Not exactly the seductive, romantic speech she'd been hoping for, but it would have to do for the moment. Her emotions were simply too high, her mouth too dry to put any of her feelings into words.

He was angry when he spoke. Surprisingly angry. Martinique didn't understand why until his words were out.

"What were you doing here?" he demanded. "I thought I told you to stay put."

Martinique felt her color rise, flushing from his unexpected accusation. She'd only wanted to help him! "I . . . I couldn't wait. I was worried. About you!"

He stepped forward, taking her by the shoulders, almost shaking her in his own effort to explain. "Worried! Hell, woman, you don't know what worry is! How do you think I felt when that creep had a hold of you again?"

Martinique had a sudden flash of insight as the meaning of his words started to sink in. She knew he'd been afraid for her. So afraid, he had to be feeling some of the same things for her that she was for him. He just didn't realize it. Yet. And just like her, he probably wasn't sure how to show it.

"How *did* you feel?" she asked him softly, holding her ground, not moving an inch out of his arms. "Maybe we both need to understand."

The question took Cade completely by surprise. Still holding Nick by the shoulders, still shuddering from the memory of what had almost happened to her, he looked into her eyes, trying to make some sense of what she was asking. But the answer formulated itself in his mind before he even realized it. He knew what he'd felt for her.

Fear. Cold, gut-wrenching terror. It was such an unfamiliar sensation to him, it had taken him a while to recognize it. But more than that, he knew what the fear for her meant. He *knew.*

He just couldn't bring himself to face it. What the hell did she want from him, anyway? He couldn't give her that. He couldn't say it out loud. If she wanted to know how he felt, actions would have to speak louder than words.

He would show her. More thoroughly, more completely than he'd ever shown a woman before. Because she was like no other woman he'd ever known.

And he was through with talking for now. Through

with figuring things out. Through with that damned rule book he'd always believed in.

Nick was wet and warm and wearing that incredibly provocative robe he'd first seen her in. The same sinfully sweet Angel-face who'd held his head in her lap. Only he'd finally returned the favor and saved her back. Hadn't he rescued her from Picasso's evil clutches? Didn't a man deserve a reward like her, just once in his life?

Why shouldn't he make love to her tonight? *Why shouldn't he?*

Unable to think of a single rational reason not to, he scooped her up in his arms and carried her into the bedroom.

ELEVEN

Nick reached up to touch Cade's face the moment they entered the room. It was an innocent gesture, he realized. One soft, tender stroke from her fingertips, but he felt the effects of it rocketing all the way down to his groin. He couldn't believe the searing pleasure it brought him, just to have Nick's hand caress him there. He caught her by the wrist and drew those fluttering fingers to his lips, kissing the sensitive tips that held the power to arouse him so completely.

"I wanted this," she whispered, her eyes wet as they gazed up at him, two liquid, limpid pools of pure desire. "I . . . prepared for it."

Her arm reached out, gesturing to the room around them, bringing the environment into focus for him for the first time. His nostrils flared as he caught the scent of herbs and flowers, mingled subtly with the heady, exquisite scent of her. The candles clustered beside the bed gave him the final clue. She'd planned the perfect seduction scene, just for him, turning her bedroom into a mystical bower for the crazy magic of their lovemaking.

He smiled at the amazing irony of it. At the disconcerting thought of Sweetness seducing *him*. Didn't she realize that he was lost to her charms already? Beyond hope where she was concerned? All she had to do was crook her little finger and he would follow. Anytime. Anywhere. Any way she wanted.

He set her down gently so that she stood in front of him beside the bed. He wanted to give her more control this time, more free will in what they were about to do. If that meant going ahead with the bewitching fantasy she'd planned, so be it.

A man had to make sacrifices every now and then to please the woman he wanted. And it wasn't exactly tough to figure out just what this one had in mind. The only hard part would be holding himself back while she showed him. Yes, that was going to be the very, *very* hard part.

"Show me, *chérie*," he said hoarsely. "Fill me in on all your secrets."

She turned the lights off in the room then, flooding them both in darkness. A match flared in the midst of the shadows, and Nick lit the candles, one by one. And then she turned to him, her figure silhouetted by a soft glow, and set his insides on fire.

One look, one hint of what she was about to do, and desire inflamed him, hotter than the flickering firelight. Holding his gaze, she toyed with the tip of the fabric belt that held her robe together. His mind flashed back to that other time when he'd prayed for that robe to open. Tonight he found himself praying for mercy.

Because he knew she was going to take it off. Any second now. *She was going to strip for him.* And he knew it was going to kill him.

She was an amateur at it, he realized. A rank, scared, very slow-going amateur. But somehow that only made the show more interesting. More exciting. Muscles fisted hard in his groin, rampantly tightening with every trembling move she made.

He was fully aroused before she even had the belt off.

She didn't swing her hips or flash some skin the way the club dancers were inclined to do. She wasn't performing. She was living the experience, feeling her way through it, one sensual, mind-blowing move at a time. And she was taking him right along with her.

Straight to paradise.

The robe whispered open when she moved, fascinating him beyond belief. He saw the hollowed cleft between her breasts, the enthralling mound of dark hair that crowned her thighs. He found himself fighting for air.

And then she drew the robe back completely, dropping it across her shoulders, displaying the rest of herself to his sight. Her body glowed from the dancing candlelight, from fear and excitement, from anticipation. His gaze settled on her swollen breasts, on the dark, peaking centers, remembering how they had tasted in his mouth. How they would taste again, tonight, when she decided to let him near enough.

He wasn't sure he could wait for that decision.

She wet her lips with her tongue, hesitating, driving him wild with waiting. The robe slipped to the floor in a soft pile. And Nick was completely naked.

She didn't look like a seductress standing there. She looked like the angel he first remembered, sent straight from heaven to save him. Every sweet, saintly, virginal inch of her made to rescue a man from his personal purgatory and give him good reason to mend his ways. God yes, the Almighty worked in mysterious ways.

Cade swore softly, marveling at the miracle of it.

"Your turn," she said shakily. "But this time I'm going to help *you* get naked."

Cade heard himself groan as she approached him slowly and started to tug at his T-shirt. Her hand stole softly across his chest, burning straight through to his heart and soul. One touch from her and every muscle he had went instantly hard. Painfully, potently hard.

He arched his back, helping her a little, and the T-shirt came free with a final tug. He kicked his shoes off next, but when she reached down to help him unzip his fly, he captured her hand and guided it to his groin, to the raging spot where his energy was strongest.

The gasp she gave sent a spear of pleasure shafting straight to that spot. But having her touch him there was simply too sweet, too intense. He had to pull her hand away. "Not now, angel-face," he said. "Not yet."

She smiled up at him. "Not until you've made *me* crazy, you mean. Why won't you let me get *you* out of control?"

"Sweetness," he said on a hoarse, throaty whisper,

"you already have." He proceeded to show her, dropping his pants to the floor, freeing that hardened part of him, the source of so much heat and energy, revealing just how little control he had left.

Martinique felt her pulse skyrocket with excitement. God, but she was grateful she hadn't used those two passion drops from Adora after all. Looking at what she'd already done to Cade, she knew they would *never* be necessary with such a virile man.

He was naked now, stripped to the skin except for the small gold ring glinting in the hollow of his stomach plane. It was just the sort of racy adornment that suited him, she realized. A daring mark, faintly piratical, modern and ancient at once. The subtle flash of metal in the candlelight caught her gaze, throwing his bare, suntanned flesh into sharp contrast, drawing her attention irresistibly downward.

To a spot below the golden jewel that was far more fascinating. Until this moment she hadn't realized just how large, how strangely frightening a fully erect male could be. Cade was the first man she'd ever seen in this condition, after all. Last time he'd been naked, she hadn't had the nerve to study him so boldly. This time she almost wished she hadn't.

Lord, but he was massive. And when she suddenly realized exactly what he was going to do to her, her knees nearly gave out from under her. She wanted it to happen. She really did. She just couldn't imagine that it wasn't going to *hurt*.

She nearly lost her nerve at that point, taking a step back from him. But Cade seemed to understand exactly how she felt. He scooped her up in his arms again and carried her to the bed, taking complete control.

"Don't worry, *chérie*," he said, his voice low and hoarse, reassuring. "I would never, never hurt you. You don't have to be afraid."

The satin sheets were cool and silky against her skin as he laid her down against them. But that was nothing compared to the sensation of his mouth on her throat. He was kissing her there, just behind the ear, murmuring something in French she could almost make out.

But if there were any doubts left in her mind as to what his meaning was, Cade's hands were saying it for him. He was stroking her everywhere, irresistibly, expertly, making her forget everything around her except the sweet shock of contact when their two bodies touched. His mouth was on her breasts, taking each erect center between his lips, tugging and teasing with the edge of his teeth.

Martinique moaned beneath him, arching at the sharp, soaring pleasure he brought her with every sweet, rhythmic slide of his tongue. His mouth moved gradually downward, kissing the soft muscles of her belly that had already begun to tighten at his touch. Instinctively, her legs had drawn together, afraid to expose the most vulnerable part of her. But in another moment he was kneeling on the floor before her, asking her to do just that.

He pressed his lips to each thigh, his kisses erotic, incredibly private. "Open your legs, *chérie*," he whispered. "And let me kiss you there too."

Martinique exhaled slowly, half in shock just from

the thought of what he wanted to do. It was the most unspeakably intimate act she could imagine. And it would leave her so wide open. So helpless.

"Come on, sweetness," he urged. "Do it."

Anticipation leapt within her as her stomach muscles clutched. She closed her eyes then, compelled to follow his forbidden lead. She felt her heart go crazy as his hands slowly spread her thighs. But when his mouth found the very center of her being, she thought her heart would stop.

She felt his lips, his tongue exploring there, searching for all of her secrets. Never had she been so electrified, so suddenly and completely aware of her own body. The pleasure was so sweet, so overwhelming, all sense of shame left her. She moved in unison with him, wild and wanton as his mouth moved deeper, tasting and sampling until she thought she would die of desire. Until her sharp, clutching cries were the only sound in the room.

"*Please,*" she moaned, soaring with the most ecstatic need she'd ever known. "Please, Cade."

He stood then, taking just a few urgent seconds to protect them both. Next thing Martinique knew, the waiting was over.

He slid her back against the sheets, bringing their bodies together so smoothly, so quickly, she barely had time to be afraid. She felt a faint piercing pain as he entered her, but the pleasure that followed filled her so completely, the tiny twinge of soreness was soon driven away. He was deep inside her, plunging and rocking rhythmically, infusing her with shafts of sensation that went straight to her soul.

She was over the edge in seconds, climaxing like crazy as he caught her up in his arms.

Cade wasn't sure if the cries he'd heard were Nick's or his own. He wasn't sure of anything at the moment except the driving, reckless need for his own release. He'd been holding himself back on purpose, fighting to keep control until Angel-face had caught her own glimpse of heaven.

The sound of her soft moans incited him to a whole new height. Her peaking brought him such astonishing satisfaction, he was shaken to the core of his soul. He was drugged with it, driven to impale himself so deeply in her throbbing, clutching flesh, his own survival was at stake. Seconds later he surrendered everything, in the most surging, shuddering climax of ecstasy and emotion he'd ever experienced.

He was lost inside her, unsure of where his own body ended and hers began. The power of it left them both shaken, gathered together as tightly as two beings could be, hanging on to each other for breath, for support, for life. The kiss they shared afterward, deep, and devastating in its intensity, was almost as shattering as the lovemaking itself.

Hugging Nick hard against him, Cade felt the tears of joy streaming down her cheeks.

"I love you," she told him, caught up in the overwhelming emotion of the moment. "I love you," she repeated simply, laying her head against his chest, settling herself comfortably in the circle of his arms.

Cade continued holding her gently, his arms locked securely around her, not quite wanting to let go. But at the same time, his gut had gone completely cold. He'd heard her words clearly. Heard them and felt his heart stop as their meaning slowly started sinking in. Felt his whole body freeze with sudden shock and uncertainty.

For once in his life he had no idea how to respond to such an unexpected, totally unfamiliar situation. He was downright clueless about what to do or say. Whole-hog terrified by her tender words.

Luckily, Nick didn't seem to need an answer. She looked so content, so satiated, and so unaware of his reaction, she gave no hint about wanting to talk any further. Shortly, very shortly, she fell asleep.

And Cade continued lying there, wide awake for most of the night, wondering exactly what to do next.

The morning felt glorious to Martinique when she finally woke. Sunlight filtered warmly through her long lace curtains, sending finely patterned shadows streaming against the far wall of her room. A lush, sultry perfume still filled the air, steamy and lingering like the early mist outside. Even her senses were overripe, flooded to capacity from the sheer fulfillment of the night before.

She was sore in places she couldn't name, wonderfully sore and damp and messy from lovemaking. Delightfully overdosed from an excess of Cade Jackson. She turned to his side of the bed, to study the man who had shared so much intimacy, who had brought her such indescribable joy.

But he was gone.

Gone?

She sat up in bed, dizzy and light-headed, trying to ignore the sick, sinking feeling that was settling in the pit of her stomach. He'd probably just left to get some breakfast, she rationalized hopefully, glancing quickly around the room, noting there wasn't a single sign of his presence left. No jeans, no boots, nothing.

Not even a note.

God, this just couldn't be happening to her, could it? She thought of running to the front window, to see if his motorcycle was still there, or checking downstairs, just in case he'd left a letter that would explain everything. But it wasn't necessary for her to get up and look. She knew where he'd gone.

Dear Lord, she *knew*.

She felt it with a calm, creeping sense of certainty, without searching the room or the apartment any further. It was like a sixth sense she'd developed overnight, a sense of incompleteness without him. An aching void inside her at his absence. She didn't have to look for him to know he'd left her.

At the first possible opportunity. Not long after they'd made love. Most likely before the day had even dawned.

Gone, she repeated silently, clutching hard at the sheets with both hands just as the pain began to hit her. She tried to gauge it dispassionately, wondering how much she would be able to take, wondering at what point it was going to kill her. The agony that seized her heart was so unbearable, she seriously doubted she could survive it.

But something broke deep inside her as soon as the first wave of it washed over her. She was laughing then, a little hysterically, laughing and crying at the cruel irony of the situation. She was a true Duval woman after all. No different from Angelé. No better than any of her brazen, beautiful, man-crazy ancestors.

In spite of her best efforts not to, she'd still fallen in love. Completely, hopelessly, recklessly in love. She'd been cautious all her life, and it still hadn't saved her from the force of fate. From the force of Cade Jackson, Cupid's secret weapon in cruel, Cajun disguise.

She'd given him everything she had. Shared her bed, her body, bared her soul to a man who'd deserted her so fast, it made her head spin.

So why had she expected it to be different between the two of them? Why had she hoped to avoid Angelé's mistakes and ended up making an even bigger one of her own? At least her mother had been able to console herself with more than one man. But Martinique knew, she *knew*, she would never find comfort with anyone else.

God, but she was an idiot a hundred times over. She'd known what kind of man Cade was. A lone wolf. Free, without any real sense of place or permanence. A man who was always on the road.

She'd been fool enough to think her love might change his mind about that kind of life. She'd been fool enough to think he might stay.

Still sitting up in bed, the bed that had sheltered so much happiness the night before, she dropped her head in her hands and let the tears start to flow. But after half an hour of solid crying, she knew the weeping wasn't going to do her any good. It certainly wasn't going to bring him back. And she still had to go on somehow, to stop feeling sorry for herself.

She showered and dressed in a daze, reminding herself she wasn't the first woman who'd ever been dumped so abruptly. If they could live through it, there was still hope for her. She'd been strong all her life, hadn't she?

Strong for her mother at first, looking after both of them in that dingy little above-bar apartment. Strong for herself when she'd been on her own.

But this. This was like no challenge she'd ever known. Like no obstacle she'd ever met up with.

Was this how Angelé had felt, time after time? This searing, aching, longing for a man she loved? Was this what it had been like for her mother?

No wonder, she thought, marveling at just how many times her mom had struggled through it. *No wonder Angelé had struggled so desperately for love.*

Something very close to forgiveness started to form in Martinique's mind. Forgiveness of her mother for her irresponsible behavior. For the dangerous, very destructive way she'd always responded to heartbreak.

If her mother's pain had been anything close to this, she could begin to understand that behavior. She could begin to let the past go for good.

As for her own feelings? If she were completely honest with herself, she'd have to admit she was still deeply in love with Cade. Even now, even after he'd left her. Somehow she knew she always would be.

Cade throttled his Harley up to full speed, heading straight for the highway. Straight back to the road and the safe, shoddy, one-person shack where he belonged.

She loved him.

The minute she'd said it, he'd known it was time to leave. Hell, it was past time. Too late to take off cleanly, without making a major, complicated mess of things. Too late to leave without hurting her.

Not that he was doing exactly fine himself. He was sick as the devil over this whole bloody business. Dangerously close to puking his guts out.

His stomach felt as slimy as buzzard saliva. Worse than that morning he'd first met Nick and involuntarily lost his lunch. He deserved to be sick again, now. He deserved the worst for deserting her.

Just living with himself might be bad enough. He was the lowest form of life he could think of at the moment. Cade Jackson, he decided, was pure, stinking pond scum.

And she *loved* him.

Loved *him?* Didn't she understand what kind of a man he was? Correction, what kind of a snake?

For the first time in his life someone had said those three amazing words to him and actually *meant* it. Someone trusting and innocent and terrific.

Someone far too good for him.

And how had he reacted? Like a yellowbelly. Like a quaking, no-kneed, spineless invertebrate. So low on the food chain, he didn't even have a tail to tuck between his legs.

But what else could he do? Stay with her? He couldn't promise to remain while his life was on the road.

A bounty hunter like him, always away from home, would make a very bad husband. It was a rough and risky profession. Probably worse than being a police officer. And he still remembered, all too clearly, how much Rand's pregnant widow had suffered after her husband's shooting.

Lori had been devastated. Understandably so. So shaken up by the loss that her baby had been born three months early.

And even though she'd been like a sister to him, Cade hadn't found any way to comfort her. The best he'd been able to do was track down the perp responsible for Rand's death and put him back in jail.

Luckily, Lori had had a tight family to look after her. Luckily, no one had needed to look after *him*. No one except the bail jumpers, that is. No one but the bad guys who'd learned to keep a lookout over their shoulders, just to see if Cade Jackson was following a few short steps behind them.

The sight of his cabin, rising from the bayou in a familiar silhouette, brought Cade out of his painful guilt-fest and back to a safer sense of reality. Temporarily. Somehow, being inside the shack again just didn't seem the same.

There were too many memories of Nick here now. Too many graphic reminders. The shower out back. The table inside. The sheets still full of her perfume.

He'd never realized before just how decrepit the place really was. How empty. A man's home might be his castle, but without a woman in it, this one was little more than a hovel. Without his Angel-face, that is.

Was this really all that his life amounted to? This bleak little box and a future filled with more of the same? More chasing. More running.

All this time, he'd thought that the crooks were the ones who'd been running away. Now, alone with his thoughts, alone with his conscience, he began to wonder. Could he honestly say that the bad guys were the only ones afraid to look behind them?

Maybe he wasn't the hunter after all. Maybe, all along, *he'd* been the one trying to escape.

From the past. From the pain. Whatever he was fleeing, it seemed to be catching up with him. This time his survival techniques didn't seem to be working.

He'd never done that kind of thing to a woman before. Yeah, he'd left a few behind, but not like that. With Sweetness, he'd simply deserted her. *He'd run away.*

It was impossible to call it anything else. And impossible to deny just how familiar it felt. Had he been high-tailing it away from his problems all along? Hell, leaving her the way he had, he couldn't even fool himself into believing his reasons for running had been right.

He had to think twice about his life this time, about the things he thought he'd stood for. To reconsider what the whole thing was about. Tracking, or making tracks. He wasn't so sure.

Maybe it was time to find out, to make a change. This shack could sure use one. Maybe he should finally get around to sprucing the place up, possibly ordering some real furniture for himself. Like a couch and a chair. And a few throw pillows.

Maybe he should get the hell out of this crappy little hole-in-the-wall and hit the nearest bar before he completely lost his mind.

Back on his bike, he headed for the honky-tonk again. But there wasn't much happening on a Monday afternoon. And the stiff belt of whiskey he downed didn't help a bit to obliterate the ache inside him. He doubted a whole bottle of it would do the trick this time.

When the bar fight that broke out in the back pool room barely held his interest, he knew he was in serious trouble.

He couldn't get her off his mind.

And he couldn't run anymore. He *wouldn't* run.

So maybe it *was* time to make a change. Maybe it was past time. But the change he was considering was a little more complex than buying furniture.

It was just crazy enough to keep him interested *and* keep him in line for the rest of his life. Crazy enough to work.

Meanwhile he had to do something. Something he hadn't done since Rand died.

He had to stop for once and turn around to face exactly what was after him.

TWELVE

"Nikki, honey . . . you okay?"

Adora's dark eyes peered intently through the morning sunlight that flooded the sidewalk down Royal Street, searching Martinique's face with more than her usual amount of concern. "You going zombie on me again, girl?"

Martinique snapped herself out of her daydream trance and reluctantly left her garbage can at the curb for the truck to collect later. Gratefully, she allowed Adora's arm to slip around her for support. There was little need to tell her all-seeing housekeeper and faithful friend that she'd been thinking about him again. About the hardheaded heartbreaker she'd discovered during trash pickup just two weeks before.

Waste disposal day, she thought ruefully, would never be the same again.

"I am *not* 'going zombie,' " she insisted, forcing her

chin up, willing the corners of her mouth into a compla-
cent smile.

If Adora had any idea how bad she really felt, there
was no end to the number of cures she might start con-
cocting. Spirit Soup, Gris-Gris Gumbo, Snake's-
Tongue Bouillabaisse. None of them sounded terribly
appetizing, especially at this time of the morning. None
of them were going to work.

"I'm just a little distracted," she added. "It's inven-
tory time in the shop. There's so much to do. I'll probably be working late again."

"Hrrrumph!" Adora grumbled, her wise, beautifully
weathered face fixed in a stern, skeptical stare. "Nice
try, Nikki girl. Your Mimi assistant, she possibly gullible
enough to buy *that* excuse. Not *me*. I *know* what's on
your mind."

"Coffee," Martinique told her with an apologetic
smile. "A nice cup of your chicory coffee should make
everything fine again."

"Bah!" Adora snorted on their way into the kitchen.
"I'll make you some coffee, all right. I'll make it good
and strong and *hot*. And then I'm gonna find that cowboy and pour it straight down his pants."

"You wouldn't!" Martinique exclaimed, smiling in
spite of herself. "You'd never find him anyway," she
added. "He's long gone."

"But not forgotten," Adora breathed cryptically.
"Come on, Nikki, why won't you let me make up a nice
little doll for you? I make it look just like him. Dark
hair, dressed in denim. Maybe wearing some itty-bitty
boots . . ."

"With straight pins in all the right places?" Martinique asked, shaking her head. "I appreciate the offer," she added. "I think. But I told you before, I don't want to hurt him."

"Won't hurt him *that* much," Adora capitulated. "Just a little."

"Not at all," Martinique said, still shaking her head. "Promise."

"Okay, Nikki," Adora finally agreed, sniffing reluctantly. "But if he ever sets foot round here again . . ."

"He won't," she responded, cutting off the one line of thought she could never allow herself to indulge in. "He wouldn't dare."

But two hours later, when Cade's motorcycle roared up outside her shop, Martinique realized she'd been wrong. Cowboy Jackson had more nerve than any man she knew. More irritating, insolent audacity than any one person had a right to.

It had been nearly a week since he'd left her, yet he still had the guts to come calling. What did he want from her now, anyway? A little more of her heart maybe? A little more of her soul? Hadn't he wounded her enough already?

When he stepped over the threshold of her store, she had half a mind to scream for Adora and give her the go-ahead on that useful little voodoo doll. She *did* want to hurt him at this moment. A few pins poked strategically into that hard, perfect body of his would be nothing compared to the pain throbbing through hers.

Just one look at him and her insides ached.

"Get out," she said, incredibly calm.

It was amazing what anger and adrenaline could do to keep a person going in a crisis, she realized. But Cade Jackson was worse than a crisis, standing there looking bold and windblown, sexy and unbridled. He was an all-out emergency. And it was going to take everything she had in her, every last ounce of strength she could muster, just to survive him.

"No," he told her, folding his arms across that beautifully broad chest, refusing to budge even an inch. He looked every bit the hard, handsome outlaw who had haunted her dreams for almost a week now. Every bit the dangerous, dark-haired bandit who'd stolen her heart.

"Fine." She picked up the phone, punching in digits with a hand that hardly trembled. What *were* those numbers again? Nine-oh-one? Nine-nine-one? This was exactly what she should've done on that first fateful morning she'd met him. Called for the cops, called for an ambulance, called for *anyone* to come and carry him away.

Striding forward, he plucked the receiver from her hand and cradled it. "That's not going to work, Nick. Nobody's dragging me out of here until we talk."

She folded her arms across her chest, mirroring his stance, tilting her chin at him. "Oh? Guess you haven't seen Adora when she's angry. If she finds you in here, you're liable to be sacrificed. To the beat of talking jungle drums. *Parts* of you can always be removed later."

"She's mad at me, too, huh?"

"Too?" Martinique asked coldly, arching her eyebrows in what she hoped was a very good imitation of indifference. "*I'm* not mad. I just want you to go."

"Tough." He advanced toward her, slow and menacing, backing her firmly, inexorably up against the far wall of her shop. Planting one hand on either side of her, he brought his face close to hers. So close, she couldn't do anything but stare into those awful, incredible, black-lashed blue eyes.

His breath was cool as crème de menthe, whispering seductively, deliciously across her lips as he spoke. "I'm not leaving until you hear me out."

God, but it really wasn't fair of him to smell the way he did. Of wind and leather and vibrant, virile maleness. Just the proximity of him left her senses overflowing, her pulse pounding wildly in her ears.

She closed her eyes, trying to block him out, to summon up what little strength she had left. "Nothing you say," she whispered quietly, rationally, "is going to make any difference."

He didn't respond immediately, and Martinique opened her eyes again, gauging his reaction. It was different than she'd imagined. More devastating. The raw, resigned expression on his face made her feel as if she'd slapped him.

He stepped back from the wall, releasing her, running his hands through his hair in frustration, as though he had no idea what to do next. It was the first time Martinique had ever seen him at a loss for action.

"I guess 'sorry' isn't going to cut it, then," he said hoarsely, fighting to get each word out.

"*Are* you sorry?" she asked, skeptically, empathizing with his agony in spite of herself.

"Very," he ground out, his voice rough.

Martinique wasn't sure what to say. She knew he was sincere. She knew it had taken a lot for him to come here and tell her that. But she also knew it wasn't enough.

He'd hurt her. A *lot*.

And while she might find it inside herself to forgive him for it, she was a different woman now from the one he'd left the week before. That woman might've taken him back on any terms. This one had learned to expect better for herself.

"Okay," she said, keeping her voice level—or trying to anyway. "Apology accepted. Now, please go."

"I will," he promised, seating himself on the edge of her sofa and dropping his head in his hands. "As soon as you let me explain. *Please*, Nick," he added, his voice deep, almost desperate. "I want you to know why I left."

"It's obvious, isn't it?" she asked, still pressed against the wall by her own will, hoping it would continue to hold her up.

"It's not what you think." He lifted his head, facing her squarely as he spoke. "It was what you said to me that night. It scared the hell out of me."

"*I* scared *you?*" she asked, incredulous. "Good one, Jackson. Whiskey bottles and bullets don't frighten you a bit, but when someone loves you, *that's* lethal?"

"Pretty stupid, huh, sweetness?"

"I am *not* your sweetness."

"Sorry, Nick. No, *Ms*. Duval," he added on the hint

of a bitter smile. "What I meant to say is, no one's ever paid me that kind of a compliment. I want you to know I'm grateful for it."

"Grateful?" she repeated, her temper rising again at his truly terrible selection of words. "There's no need to be, I promise. Whatever I feel for you is completely involuntary. If I'd had a choice, I would've picked someone like Dennis Harold instead."

"That goon without the hair?" he asked, apparently insulted. "I'm getting a little tired of that guy. He'd better not get within a mile of you again."

Martinique felt herself growing angrier by the minute. "I don't see what you have to say about it."

"Plenty." Cade fired up to his feet again, towering over her against the wall. "I have plenty left to say about that," he insisted, taking her chin in his hands, forcing her to meet his gaze. "You see, sweetness, I love you too."

Martinique's heart crowded into her throat at the sound of his words, almost taking her breath away. *He loved her?*

He loved her!

God, but it was a beautiful thing to hear. Beautiful and heartbreaking. Because it still wasn't enough.

She needed more than words from the man in her life, whoever he turned out to be. She needed long-lasting loyalty and total trust. Someone who was willing to stick around. Forever. For always.

Maybe she was the one who should be grateful to him. For teaching her so much about herself. She'd learned she was like Angelé in a lot of ways. But the fatal flaw she'd been afraid of inheriting from her female ancestors wasn't a flaw at all.

It was a gift. An incredible capacity to love someone completely.

But any other similarities she shared with her relatives ended right there. Unlike Angelé, she knew she deserved to be loved back. Just as fully as she loved, and just as passionately. With nothing less than a lifelong commitment.

Her hand reached up gently to touch Cade on the cheek. She loved him still, more than ever. But it wasn't going to change what she had to say. There wasn't any way to avoid the pain she might be bringing them both. The agony.

Because she knew the time had finally come to tell him good-bye. For good. For bad. Forever.

Tears crowded behind her eyes, sharp and stinging. "I'm sorry," she whispered softly. "But even if there is love between us, for both of us, it's still not going to work."

Cade felt his face going white at her words, every last drop of blood draining straight to his gut. He'd never let himself believe it was hopeless. He'd somehow hung on to the idea that Nick might find it in her heart to forgive him. Yet here he was, in love with her, and she was still telling him to get lost.

The fact that he deserved to be dumped by her didn't make his landing any softer. The rip at his heart was brutal, wrenching. He pulled away from her, turning his back so that she couldn't read the intensity of the blow she'd dealt him.

"Unless," she added quietly behind him, "you're ready to make me a promise. Some kind of commitment that says you're willing to stay. I have to be able to count on the fact that you want to stick around. I have to be able to count on *you*."

Cade whipped back around to face her again, ready to sink to his knees in front of her. He *did* sink to his knees.

"Be my wife, Nick," he said simply. "And I'll never leave again. Never."

The surprise on her face made him smile. "I'm dead serious," he assured her.

"Don't *do* this," she begged, tugging at his hands, urging him up again. "Unless you really mean it. From everything I know about you so far, it's hard to imagine you want to be tied down. That grudge of yours against the world, that chip on your shoulder the size of a small mountain, is what keeps you going. And it seems impossible to me that you're ever going to be completely rid of it."

"I thought so too," he told her. "For a long time. But I've been working on it, babe. Back at the shack, for starters. It's amazing how clear things can get in a man's mind when he's all alone. So alone, the walls start closing in on him and he has nothing to do but face his own demons. And evaluate his life. Believe me, Nick, I didn't like a lot of what I saw in the past. But it was the road ahead that really scared the socks off me."

"The future?" she asked.

"The solitude," he explained. "A life with no one. No one to be responsible for except myself. No one to come home to. And no end in sight. It looked pretty damn awful, angel-face. I had to get out of there. I finally decided to go talk to someone. Someone who confirmed exactly what I'd been thinking and wisely convinced me what a fool I was."

"Who?" she asked, still hanging on to his hands as if she would never let go.

Cade walked her over to the sofa and settled them both down before he started to explain. "My ex-partner's widow, Lori."

Martinique nodded slowly. "I remember you mentioning her before. I didn't realize you were still close."

"We weren't," he admitted bluntly. "I hadn't been able to face her since Rand died. Some brave bounty hunter I am, huh? Guess I just cave around good women."

"You were grieving," she said gently. "You'd lost your best friend."

His voice grew hoarse. "In a way, I'd always felt partly to blame for his death. Like I should've been the one who took the bullet. I never knew how to tell Lori that. I knew there was no way I could help her."

"Did you help her now?" Nick asked.

He shook his head, thoughtful. "She helped me instead. Guess I was the one who really needed it. She's moved on with her life. Has a new husband, two kids, the whole thing. Says Rand would've wanted it that way. Would've wanted us both to find some happiness without him."

"I'm sure that's what you would've wanted for him," she said gently, "if it had been the other way around."

He squeezed her hands hard, then let them go, standing to pace restlessly across the length of her small, very compact shop. "Don't you see, Nick? I *did* want it the other way around. I wished I'd been the one who died. I didn't have anyone to leave behind like he did. And afterwards, I had nothing to be afraid of, no reason to stop running."

He halted in front of her, hooking two fingers in the belt loops of his blue jeans, shooting her a direct, disarming stare. "Until I met you."

"Are you saying it's different now? That you're really going to stop and settle down somewhere?"

"With *someone*," he corrected. "I'm ready to try. No, more than that. I'm ready to make it work."

"With me?"

"Definitely with you, *chérie*. Only with you. When I went back to my cabin and tried to go on there again without you, it hit me hard just how much I was giving up. How many years of a real life I'd already sacrificed for the sake of vengeance."

Martinique studied him thoughtfully. "They say revenge can be sweet."

"Very sweet," he agreed. "But it's a dish best served cold. And the ice is gone from inside me, sweetness. Melted by you."

"I did that?" she asked, a little in awe. "But—"

"Before you ask," he continued, reading her thoughts, "the answer is no. I don't ever want that kind of bitterness back. Sure, the anger gave me an edge in the game. But staying that way indefinitely takes too much of a man's energy. Drains him until there's nothing left. I'd just as soon lay off before it's too late. Get a life of my own. With you if you'll have me."

Martinique wanted to say yes. She wanted it like crazy. But the thought of being married to a biker bounty-hunter still troubled her. Because with a dangerous job like that, she knew she would always be worried about him. "What about your career?" she asked. "Think you could ever get used to doing something else? *Anything* that involves a desk or an office?"

"Sorry, sweetness." He kissed her on the forehead, dropping back down beside her on the sofa. "But you're never going to turn me into a pencil pusher."

"No way, huh?"

"No way. But I have been thinking about starting my own security business. Something that won't keep me on the road constantly. Something that will help protect folks before the bad guys get to them."

"Here?" she asked hopefully. "In town?"

"Sure," he agreed. "Creeps are crashing out on innocent victims' sidewalks all the time in this city. Something should be done about it, don't you think? I have to go where I'm needed."

"You are needed here," she whispered. "Right here."

"*Chérie*," he said, cradling her face gently between his hands. "Does this mean you'll marry me?"

Martinique stared into his eyes, sinking irretrievably into the bayou blue depths. She could get lost in them forever, she realized. But did she dare? Was she ready to risk taking him back again, to trust him totally with her love, with her life?

There was something different when she looked deep into his soul this time. A kind of solemn patience and hope for the future that hadn't been there before. He really was in earnest about this whole thing, about the two of them spending eternity together.

Knowing just how stubborn he could be when he set his mind on something, how determined and positively pigheaded, Martinique realized she could count on him to follow through. If she agreed to marry him, she knew she'd never be rid of him. Thank goodness. Because she couldn't think of anything she'd ever wanted more than to be his wife.

"Yes," she finally told him. "I'll marry you."

He was crushing her to him before she could get all the words out. "Thank God, angel-face," he said roughly, his hands on her shoulders, her hair, everywhere. "You really had me scared there for a while. I thought I'd lost you."

He bent to take her lips with his, and Martinique felt the hard strength and heat of him slowly enveloping her, surrounding her with pure protective warmth and passion. Never in her life, not even in childhood, had she felt so wonderfully safe, so completely secure. She'd finally found it at last, that elusive sense of belonging she'd been searching for all her life.

He deepened the kiss, suddenly taking her sense of elation to a whole new level. She was caught up in the lazy, languorous sensuality of his mouth on hers, his tongue tasting her in slow erotic ways he'd never tried before. There was nothing safe about what his hands were doing to her either, cupping her breasts, her bottom, with a daring audacity that could only be described as possessive.

She moaned softly, realizing that this part of their life would never be riskless or secure. Lovemaking with Cade would always be slightly perilous and unexpected, exquisitely unpredictable. She gave a second cry, sweetly shocked. She wasn't even aware she'd done it until he came up for air.

"Mmmm, sweetness," he groaned, "those sounds you make do dangerous things to me."

"Good," she said shakily. "I think I'm going to like living on the edge."

He grew serious for a moment, holding her away from him at a safe distance. "That may be *how* we're going to live, but I've been giving some thought as to *where*."

"Uh-oh," she said, trying to look serious herself. "Don't tell me. You *do* want me to redecorate the shack."

"I don't want you to touch it," he told her. "Too many good memories. I might agree to hot water and electricity, though, in case we ever want to use it as a weekend getaway."

"It *is* pretty out there," she agreed. "But I'm honestly relieved you don't have any intentions of living in that cabin. Why don't you move in here after we're married?"

Cade lifted his dark eyebrows in surprise, his handsome face teasing and terrified with mock horror. "Are you kidding?" he asked. "And have that woman of yours shooting daggers at me all the time? She's liable to hex me out of the house."

Martinique laughed at that. "Well, she *did* offer to make a doll in your likeness. A kind of Cowboy Cade pincushion."

"Ouch."

"You'll be glad to know I didn't let her."

"*Very* glad."

"But wherever we live, I still expect Adora to be part of my life. She is slightly eccentric, but she's wonderful when you get to know her."

"I'll take your word for that, sweetness," he said. "She can even move in with us if you want her to. There's more than enough room where we're going."

"Where *are* we going?" she asked, suddenly curious.

"It's a secret," he whispered mysteriously, looking sexy and smug and incredibly proud of himself all at the same time. "I'll show you as soon as we set the date."

Perched on the back of Cade's bike, rocketing down the most sedate, exclusive part of St. Charles Avenue in the Garden District, Martinique couldn't imagine what the secret was. Getting there, she decided, was half the fun. The afternoon was lush with warmth, dripping with scenery and sunshine. Greek Revival and antebellum mansions swept past them in an antique architectural parade, daylight dazzling off their formal lawns and fancy rose gardens, bursting forth in brilliant crystal rainbows from their long, leaded glass windows.

She'd always been awestruck by this part of the city,

not only by the amazing display of elegance and wealth but also by the sheer sense of permanence and security that pervaded each old, orderly block.

Slowing the bike to a screaming crawl as a trolley car rumbled past, Cade took a hard left turn and glided to a pinpoint stop at the second block, right in front of the biggest, most beautiful house on the whole street. Martinique stared up at the massive white columns crowned by Corinthian capitals, the wide, welcoming veranda, the glittering cut-glass windows soaring all the way to the third floor.

"Is this the surprise?" she asked, enthralled. "Are you planning to rent it for our honeymoon or something?"

"Or something," he agreed, escorting her off the bike, across the mossy green lawn, and up the gray stone front steps.

"It's empty!" she exclaimed, peering through the long glass panes on either side of the front door. "Look at that staircase. It's gorgeous." She turned back toward him, more curious than ever. "But, Cade, I don't get it. How can we stay here for a week if it isn't furnished?"

Taking a key from his back pocket, he unlocked the front door, but he wouldn't let her in just yet. "I was hoping you might want to stay a little longer than that," he said cryptically.

She smiled up at him, her heart hammering from the sensual promise that underscored his every word. "A longer honeymoon?" she asked. "I'd *love* it. As long as we can afford it. Renting this place must cost a fortune."

"Sweetness," he said patiently, gathering her into

his arms, taking her chin in his hand. "I didn't rent it. I bought it."

"You *bought* it?" she repeated.

"With cash," he confirmed. "I think the real estate lady loves me too."

Afraid her legs were going to give out from under her, Martinique sank down onto the front steps.

"You do like it, don't you?" Cade asked cautiously.

"It's stunning," she whispered. "Literally. I adore it. But how . . ."

"Can I afford it? Simple math." He settled down beside her. "Hard work combined with some serious stock investments. Remember, Nick, I've been busting bad guys for a long time. Catching crooks can be very profitable. I just never had much to spend my money on. And you *did* tell me you wanted a nice house someday."

She shook her head, still trying to recover from the overwhelming shock of it. The overwhelming joy. "Something cozy with a picket fence around it is 'nice.' This is incredible. I can't believe you bought it for—"

"Us," he finished. "Sorry it's not furnished. I thought you'd probably want to do that yourself."

She blinked at him, wide-eyed. "I—I'd like that a lot. I'd want to fill it with antiques, of course. But Cade, do you realize what that's going to take?"

"Sure," he said, shrugging. "Talent. And you've got lots of that, angel-face. It'll probably take a pile of money too. And luckily, *I've* got plenty of that."

"You never told me you were—"

"Rich?" he prompted, completing her thought. "You never asked."

"I never imagined," she breathed.

"Good thing," he told her. "Now I know you weren't chasing me for my money."

"Chasing you!" she exclaimed, punching him playfully on the arm. "You wanted me *bad*, Jackson, and you know it."

"Still do," he admitted, his eyes gleaming with a sensual, sapphire light that almost stripped the air from her lungs. "So, you think you can learn to live with me and my bank account?"

"Pretty sure," she said mischievously. "Not that I'm complaining, but don't you think the house is a little large for just the two of us?"

"Could be. But we'll have to do something about that, won't we?"

"Such as?"

"Such as filling it up with little ones."

"Oh!" she exclaimed softly, meeting the sexy, explicit look in his eyes with an innocent smile of her own. "Any idea how to go about it?"

"A few." He rose to his feet and turned back toward the front entrance. "Come on, sweetness," he said, taking her firmly by the arm, "let me show you the inside. If you think the staircase is something, you're not going to believe the master bedroom. . . ."

Martinique's breath caught as she imagined being in that bedroom with Cade, making sweet, spicy love with him for many years to come. Making love with the red-hot, reckless Cajun who'd come to recover her property and ended up stealing her heart instead. She would surrender it to him again gladly, she realized.

Heart, soul, breath, body, any part of her he cared to take. Because in capturing her dreams, he'd won them both the biggest bounty of all. The greatest reward life has to offer. Love.

THE EDITORS' CORNER

February is on the way, which can mean only one thing—it's time for Treasured Tales V! In our continuing tradition, LOVESWEPT presents four spectacular new romances inspired by age-old myths, fairy tales, and legends.

LOVESWEPT favorite Laura Taylor weaves a tapestry of love across the threads of time in **CLOUD DANCER**, LOVESWEPT #822. Smoke, flames, and a cry for help call Clayton Sloan to the rescue, but the fierce Cheyenne warrior is shocked to find himself a hero in an unknown time. Torn by fate from all that he loves, Clay is anchored only by his longing for Kelly Farrell, the brave woman who knows his secret and the torment that shadows his nights. In this breathtaking journey through history, Laura Taylor once more demonstrates her unique storytelling gifts in a moving evocation of the healing power of love.

A chance encounter turns into a passionate journey for two in **DESTINY UNKNOWN**, LOVESWEPT #823, from the talented Maris Soule. He grins at the cool beauty whose grip on a fluffy dog is about to slip, but Cody Taylor gets even more pleasure from noticing Bernadette Sanders's reaction to his down and dirty appearance. Common sense tells the sleek store executive not to get sidetracked by the glint in the maverick builder's eyes. But when he seeks her out time and time again, daring to challenge her expectations, to ignite her desire, she succumbs to her hunger for the unconventional rogue. Maris Soule demonstrates why romantic chemistry can be so deliciously explosive.

From award-winning author Suzanne Brockmann comes **OTHERWISE ENGAGED**, LOVESWEPT #824. Funny, charismatic, and one heck of a temptation, Preston Seaholm makes a wickedly sexy hero as he rescues Molly Cassidy from tumbling off the roof! The pretty widow bewitches him with a smile, unaware that the tanned sun god is Sunrise Key's mysterious tycoon—and one of the most eligible bachelors in the country. He needs her help to fend off unwanted advances, but once he's persuaded her to play along at pretending they're engaged, he finds himself helplessly surrendering to her temptation. As fast-paced and touching as it is sensual, this is another winner from Suzanne Brockmann.

Last but not least, Kathy Lynn Emerson offers a hero who learns to **LOVE THY NEIGHBOR**, LOVESWEPT #825. The moment she drives up in a flame-red Mustang to claim the crumbling house next door, Marshall Austin knows he was right. Linnea Bryan is bewitching, a fascinating puzzle who can easily hold him spellbound—but she is also the daughter of the woman who destroyed his parents' marriage. So he launches his campaign to send her packing. But even as he insists he wants her out of town by nightfall, his heart is really saying he wants her all night long. Kathy Lynn Emerson draws the battle lines, then lets the seduction begin in her LOVESWEPT debut!

Happy reading!

With warmest wishes,

Beth de Guzman

Shauna Summers

Beth de Guzman   Shauna Summers

Senior Editor   Editor

P.S. Watch for these Bantam women's fiction titles coming in February: Available for the first time in paperback is the *New York Times* bestseller **GUILTY AS SIN** by the new master of suspense, Tami Hoag. Jane Feather, author of the nationally bestselling *VICE* and *VALENTINE*, is set to thrill romance lovers once again with **THE DIAMOND SLIPPER**, a tale of passion and intrigue involving a forced bride, a reluctant hero, and a jeweled charm. And finally, from Michelle Martin comes **STOLEN HEARTS**, a contemporary romance in the tradition of Jayne Ann Krentz in which an ex–jewel thief pulls the con of her life, but one man is determined to catch her—and never let her get away. Don't miss the previews of these exceptional novels in next month's LOVE-SWEPTs. And immediately following this page, sneak a peek at the Bantam women's fiction titles on sale *now*!

For current information on Bantam's women's fiction, visit our new web site, *Isn't It Romantic*, at the following address: **http://www.bdd.com/romance**

Don't miss these terrific novels
by your favorite Bantam authors

On sale in December:

HAWK O'TOOLE'S HOSTAGE
by Sandra Brown

THE UGLY DUCKLING
by Iris Johansen

WICKED
by Susan Johnson

HEART OF THE FALCON
by Suzanne Robinson

Sandra Brown

Her heady blend of passion, humor, and high-voltage romantic suspense has made her one of the most beloved writers in America. Now the author of more than two dozen New York Times *bestsellers weaves a thrilling tale of a woman who finds herself at the mercy of a handsome stranger—and the treacherous feelings only he can arouse. . . .*

HAWK O'TOOLE'S HOSTAGE

A classic Bantam romance available in hardcover for the first time in December 1996

To Hawk O'Toole, she was a pawn in a desperate gamble to help his people. To Miranda Price, he was a stranger who'd done the unthinkable: kidnapped her and her young son from a train full of sight-seeing vacationers. Now held hostage on a distant reservation for reasons she cannot at first fathom, Miranda finds herself battling a captor who is by turns harsh and tender, mysteriously aloof, and danger-ously seductive.

Hawk assumed that Miranda, the beautiful ex-wife of Representative Price, would be as selfish and immoral as the tabloids suggested. Instead, she seems genuinely afraid for her son's life—and willing to risk her own to keep his safe. But, committed to a fight he didn't start, Hawk knows he can't afford to feel anything but contempt for his prisoner. To force the government to reopen the Lone Puma Mine, he must keep Miranda at arm's length, to remember that she is his enemy—even when she ignites his deepest desires.

Slowly, Miranda begins to learn what drives this brooding, solitary man, to discover the truth about his tragic past. But it will take a shocking revelation to finally force her to face her own past and the woman she's become . . . and to ask herself: Is it freedom she really wants . . . or the chance to stay with Hawk forever?

"Only Iris Johansen can so magically mix a love story with hair-raising adventure and suspense. Don't miss this page-turner."—Catherine Coulter

THE UGLY DUCKLING

by *New York Times* bestselling author

Iris Johansen

now available in paperback

Plain, soft-spoken Nell Calder isn't the type of woman to inspire envy, lust—or murderous passion. Until one night when the unimaginable happens, and her life, her dreams, her future, are shattered by a brutal attack. Though badly hurt, she emerges from the nightmare a woman transformed, with an exquisitely beautiful face and strong, lithe body. While Nicholas Tanek, a mysterious stranger who compels both fear and fascination, gives her a reason to go on living. But divulging the identity of her assailant to Nell might just turn out to be the biggest mistake of Tanek's life. For he will soon find his carefully laid plans jeopardized by Nell's daring to strike out on her own.

He had come for nothing, Nicholas thought in disgust as he gazed down at the surf crashing on the rocks below. No one would want to kill Nell Calder. She was no more likely to be connected with Gardeaux than that big-eyed elf she was now lavishing with French pastry and adoration.

If there was a target here, it was probably Kavinski. As head of an emerging Russian state, he had the power to be either a cash cow or extremely trouble-some to Gardeaux. Nell Calder wouldn't be consid-ered troublesome to anyone. He had known the answers to all the questions he had asked her, but he had wanted to see her reactions. He had been watch-ing her all evening, and it was clear she was a nice, shy woman, totally out of her depth even with those fairly innocuous sharks downstairs. He couldn't imagine her having enough influence to warrant bribery, and she would never have been able to deal one-on-one with Gardeaux.

Unless she was more than she appeared. Possibly. She seemed as meek as a lamb, but she'd had the guts to toss him out of her daughter's room.

Everyone fought back if the battle was important enough. And it was important for Nell Calder not to share her daughter with him. No, the list must mean something else. When he went back downstairs, he would stay close to Kavinski.

> *"Here we go up, up, up*
> *High in the sky so blue.*
> *Here we go down, down, down*
> *Touching the rose so red."*

She was singing to the kid. He had always liked lullabies. There was a reassuring continuity about them that had been missing in his own life. Since the dawn of time, mothers had sung to their children, and they would probably still be singing to them a thou-sand years from then.

The song ended with a low chuckle and a murmur he couldn't hear.

She came out of the bedroom and closed the door

a few minutes later. She was flushed and glowing with an expression as soft as melted butter.

"I've never heard that lullaby before," he said.

She looked startled, as if she'd forgotten he was still there. "It's very old. My grandmother used to sing it to me."

"Is your daughter asleep?"

"No, but she will be soon. I started the music box for her again. By the time it finishes, she usually nods off."

"She's a beautiful child."

"Yes." A luminous smile turned her plain face radiant once more. "Yes, she is."

He stared at her, intrigued. He found he wanted to keep that smile on her face. "And bright?"

"Sometimes too bright. Her imagination can be troublesome. But she's always reasonable and you can talk to—" She broke off and her eagerness faded. "But this can't interest you. I forgot the tray. I'll go back for it."

"Don't bother. You'll disturb Jill. The maid can pick it up in the morning."

She gave him a level glance. "That's what I told you."

He smiled. "But then I didn't want to listen. Now it makes perfect sense to me."

"Because it's what you want to do."

"Exactly."

"I have to go back too. I haven't met Kavinski yet." She moved toward the door.

"Wait. I think you'll want to remove that chocolate from your gown first."

"Damn." She frowned as she looked down at the stain on the skirt. "I forgot." She turned toward the bathroom and said dryly, "Go on. I assure you I don't need your help with this problem."

He hesitated.

She glanced at him pointedly over her shoulder.

He had no excuse for staying, not that that small fact would have deterred him.

But he also had no reason. He had lived by his wits too long not to trust his instincts, and this woman wasn't a target of any sort. He should be watching Kavinski.

He turned toward the door. "I'll tell the maid you're ready for her to come back."

"Thank you, that's very kind of you," she said automatically as she disappeared into the bathroom.

Good manners obviously instilled from childhood. Loyalty. Gentleness. A nice woman whose world was centered on that sweet kid. He had definitely drawn a blank.

The maid wasn't waiting in the hallway. He'd have to send up one of the servants from downstairs.

He moved quickly through the corridors and started down the staircase.

Shots.

Coming from the ballroom.

Christ.

He tore down the stairs.

WICKED

by Susan Johnson

"An exceptional writer."—*Affaire de Coeur*

Serena Blythe's plans to escape a life of servitude had gone terribly awry. So she took the only course left to her. She sneaked aboard a sleek yacht about to set sail—and found herself face-to-face with a dangerous sensual stranger. Beau St. Jules, the Earl of Rochefort, had long surpassed his father's notoriety as a libertine. Less well known was his role as intelligence-gatherer for England. Yet even on a mission to seek vital war information, he couldn't resist practicing his well-polished seduction on the beautiful, disarmingly innocent stowaway. And in the weeks to come, with battles breaking out on the Continent and Serena's life in peril, St. Jules would risk everything to rescue the one woman who'd finally captured his heart.

"Your life sounds idyllic. Unlike mine of late," Serena said with a fleeting grimace. "But I intend to change that."

Frantic warning bells went off in Beau's consciousness. Had she *deliberately* come on board? Were her designing relatives even now in hot pursuit? Or were they explaining the ruinous details to his father instead? "How exactly," he softly inquired, his dark eyes wary, "do you plan on facilitating those changes?"

"Don't be alarmed," she said, suddenly grinning. "I have no designs on you."

He laughed, his good spirits instantly restored. "Candid women have always appealed to me."

"While men with yachts are out of my league." Her smile was dazzling. "But why don't you deal us another hand," she cheerfully said, "and I'll see what I can do about mending my fortunes."

She was either completely ingenuous or the most skillful coquette. But he had more than enough money to indulge her, and she amused him immensely.

He dealt the cards.

And when the beefsteaks arrived sometime later, the cards were put away and they both tucked into the succulent meat with gusto.

She ate with a quiet intensity, absorbed in the food and the act of eating. It made him consider his casual acceptance of all the privileges in his life with a new regard. But only briefly, because he was very young, very wealthy, too handsome for complete humility, and beset by intense carnal impulses that were profoundly immune to principle.

He'd simply offer her a liberal settlement when the *Siren* docked in Naples, he thought, discarding any further moral scruples.

He glanced at the clock.

Three-thirty.

They'd be making love in the golden light of dawn . . . or sooner perhaps, he thought with a faint smile, reaching across the small table to refill her wineglass.

"This must be heaven or very near . . ." Serena murmured, looking up from cutting another portion of beefsteak. "I can't thank you enough."

"Remy deserves all the credit."

"You're very disarming. And kind."

"You're very beautiful, Miss Blythe. And a damned good card player."

"Papa practiced with me. He was an accomplished player when he wasn't drinking."

"Have you thought of making your fortune in the gaming rooms instead of wasting your time as an underpaid governess?"

"No," she softly said, her gaze direct.

"Forgive me. I meant no rudeness. But the demimonde is not without its charm."

"I'm sure it is for a man," she said, taking a squarely cut piece of steak off her fork with perfect white teeth. "However, I'm going to art school in Florence," she went on, beginning to chew. "And I shall make my living painting."

"Painting what?"

She chewed a moment more, savoring the flavors, then swallowed. "Portraits, of course. Where the money is. I shall be flattering in the extreme. I'm very good, you know."

"I'm sure you are." And he intended to find out how good she was in other ways as well. "Why don't I give you your first commission?" He'd stopped eating but he'd not stopped drinking, and he gazed at her over the rim of his wineglass.

"I don't have my paints. They're on the *Betty Lee* with my luggage."

"We could put ashore in Portugal and buy you some. How much do you charge?"

Her gaze shifted from her plate. "Nothing for you. You've been generous in the extreme. I'd be honored to paint you"—she paused and smiled—"whoever you are."

"Beau St. Jules."

"*The* Beau St. Jules?" She put her flatware down and openly studied him. "The darling of the broadsheets . . . London's premier rake who's outsinned his father, The Saint?" A note of teasing had entered her voice, a familiar, intimate reflection occasioned by the numerous glasses of wine she'd drunk. "Should I be alarmed?"

He shook his head, amusement in his eyes. "I'm very ordinary," he modestly said, this man who stood stud to all the London beauties. "You needn't be alarmed."

He wasn't ordinary, of course, not in any way. He was the gold standard, she didn't doubt, by which male beauty was judged. His perfect features and artfully cropped black hair reminded her of classic Greek sculpture; his overt masculinity, however, was much less the refined cultural ideal. He was startlingly male.

"Aren't rakes older? You're very young," she declared. And gorgeous as a young god, she decided, although the cachet of his notorious reputation probably wasn't based on his beauty alone. He was very charming.

He shrugged at her comment on his age. He'd begun his carnal amusements very young he could have said, but, circumspect, asked instead, "How old are *you?*" His smile was warm, personal. "Out in the world on your own?"

"Twenty-three." Her voice held a small defiance; a single lady of three and twenty was deemed a spinster in any society.

"A very nice age," he pleasantly noted, his dark eyes lazily half-lidded. "Do you like floating islands?"

She looked at him blankly.

"The dessert."

"Oh, yes, of course." She smiled. "I should save room then."

By all means, he licentiously thought, nodding a smiling approval, filling their wineglasses once more. *Save room for me—because I'm coming in. . . .*

Blazing with romance, intrigue, and the splendor of
ancient Egypt

HEART OF THE FALCON

The bestselling

Suzanne Robinson
at her finest

*All her life, raven-haired Anqet had basked in the tran-
quillity of Nefer . . . until the day her father died and
her uncle descended upon the estate, hungry for her land,
hungry for her. Desperate to escape his cruel obsession, she
fled. But now, masquerading as a commoner in the magnificent city of Thebes, Anqet faces a new danger. Mysterious and seductive, Count Seth seems to be a loyal soldier to
the pharaoh. Yet soon Anqet will find that he's drawn her
back into a web of treachery and desire, where one false
move could end her life and his fiery passion could brand
her soul.*

Anqet waited for the procession to pass. She had
asked for directions to the Street of the Scarab. If she
was correct, this alley would lead directly to her goal.
She followed the dusty, shaded path between win-
dowless buildings, eager to reach the house of Lady
Gasantra before dark. She hadn't eaten since leaving
her barber companion and his family earlier in the
afternoon, and her stomach rumbled noisily. She

hoped Tamit would remember her. They hadn't seen each other for several years.

The alley twisted back and forth several times, but Anqet at last saw the intersection with the Street of the Scarab. Intent upon reaching the end of her journey, she ran into the road, into the path of an oncoming chariot.

There was a shout, then the screams of outraged horses as the driver of the chariot hauled his animals back. Anqet ducked to the ground beneath pawing hooves. Swerving, the vehicle skidded and tipped. The horses reared and stamped, showering stones and dust over Anqet.

From behind the bronze-plated chariot came a stream of oaths. Someone pounced on Anqet from the vehicle, hauling her to her feet by her hair, and shaking her roughly.

"You little gutter-frog! I ought to whip you for dashing about like a demented antelope. You could have caused one of my horses to break a leg."

Anqet's head rattled on her shoulders. Surprised, she bore with this treatment for a few moments before stamping on a sandaled foot. There was a yelp. The shaking stopped, but now two strong hands gripped her wrists. Silence reigned while her attacker recovered from his pain, then a new string of obscenities rained upon her. The retort she thought up never passed her lips, for when she raised her eyes to those of the charioteer, she forgot her words.

Eyes of deep green, the color of the leaves of a water lily. Eyes weren't supposed to be green. Eyes were brown, or black, and they didn't glaze with the molten fury of the Lake of Fire in the *Book of the Dead.* Anqet stared into those pools of malachite until, at a call behind her, they shifted to look over her head.

"Count Seth! My lord, are you injured?"

"No, Dega. See to the horses while I deal with this, this . . ."

Anqet stared up at the count while he spoke to his servant. He was unlike any man she had ever seen. Tall, slender, with lean, catlike muscles, he had wide shoulders that were in perfect proportion to his flat torso and long legs. He wore a short soldier's kilt belted around his hips. A bronze corselet stretched tight across his wide chest; leather bands protected his wrists and accentuated elegant, long-fingered hands that gripped Anqet in a numbing hold. Anqet gazed back at Count Seth and noted the strange auburn tint of the silky hair that fell almost to his shoulders. He was beautiful. Exotic and beautiful, and wildly furious.

Count Seth snarled at her. "You're fortunate my team wasn't hurt, or I'd take their cost out on your hide."

Anqet's temper flared. She forgot that she was supposed to be a humble commoner. Her chin came up, her voice raised in command.

"Release me at once."

Shock made Count Seth obey the order. No woman spoke to him thus. For the first time, he really looked at the girl before him. She faced him squarely and met his gaze, not with the humility or appreciation he was used to, but with the anger of an equal.

Bareka! What an uncommonly beautiful commoner. Where in the Two Lands had she gotten those fragile features? Her face was enchanting. High-arched brows curved over enormous black eyes that glittered with highlights of brown and inspected him as if he were a stray dog.

Seth let his eyes rest for a moment on her lips. To watch them move made him want to lick them. He appraised the fullness of her breasts and the length of her legs. To his chagrin, he felt a wave of desire pulse through his veins and settle demandingly in his groin.

Curse the girl. She had stirred him past control. Well, he was never one to neglect an opportunity. What else could be expected of a barbarian half-breed?

Seth moved with the swiftness of an attacking lion, pulling the girl to him. She fit perfectly against his body. Her soft flesh made him want to thrust his hips against her, right in the middle of the street. He cursed as she squirmed against him in a futile effort to escape and further tortured his barely leashed senses.

"Release me!"

Seth uttered a light, mocking laugh. "Compose yourself, my sweet. Surely you won't mind repaying me for my inconvenience?"